I0628099

A Bronx Tale

Lock Down Publications and Ca$h
Presents
A Bronx Tale
A Novel by *Ghost*

A Bronx Tale

Lock Down Publications
P.O. Box 870494
Mesquite, Tx 75187

Visit our website @
www.lockdownpublications.com

Copyright 2019 A Bronx Tale

All rights reserved. No part of this book may be
reproduced in any form or by electronic or mechanical
means, including information storage and retrieval systems
without permission in writing from the publisher, except by a
reviewer who may quote brief passages in review.
First Edition January 2019
Printed in the United States of America

*This is a work of fiction. Names, characters, places, and
incidents either are products of the author's imagination or
are used fictitiously. Any similarity to actual events or
locales or persons, living or dead, is entirely coincidental.*

Lock Down Publications
Like our page on Facebook: Lock Down Publications
@
www.facebook.com/lockdownpublications.ldp
Cover design and layout by: **Dynasty Cover Me**
Book interior design by: **Shawn Walker**
Edited by: **Lauren Burton**

Stay Connected with Us!

Text **LOCKDOWN** to 22828 to stay up-to-date with
new releases, sneak peaks, contests and more…
Or **CLICK HERE** to sign up.
Thank you.

Like our page on Facebook:

Lock Down Publications: Facebook

Join Lock Down Publications/The New Era Reading
Group

Visit our website @
www.lockdownpublications.com

Follow us on Instagram:

Lock Down Publications: Instagram

Email Us: We want to hear from you!

Submission Guideline.

Submit the first three chapters of your completed manuscript to ldpsubmissions@gmail.com, subject line: Your book's title. The manuscript must be in a .doc file and sent as an attachment. Document should be in Times New Roman, double spaced and in size 12 font. Also, provide your synopsis and full contact information. If sending multiple submissions, they must each be in a separate email.

Have a story but no way to send it electronically? You can still submit to LDP/Ca$h Presents. Send in the first three chapters, written or typed, of your completed manuscript to:

LDP: Submissions Dept
Po Box 870494
Mesquite, Tx 75187

DO NOT send original manuscript. Must be a duplicate.

Provide your synopsis and a cover letter containing your full contact information.

Thanks for considering LDP and Ca$h Presents.

Ghost

Chapter 1

Jahmani

It felt like I was in an oven. Sweat slid down the side of my face and ran along my collarbone. The back of my shirt was sticking to me. I had to keep taking deep breaths to try to center myself. I felt like passing out in the small apartment with roaches crawling all over the floor and walls. There was one big, white roach hanging upside down on the ceiling, threatening to drop onto the table at any minute. It had an egg hanging out of its butt. Just the sight of it made me itchy. I was ready to get out of Samantha's crib.

Whenever I stopped by, I tried my best to never stay for more than fifteen minutes at a time. Her living conditions were unbearable. But she was brother's baby mother, and I had to make sure she and his five-year-old daughter, Lonnie, were good while he was away serving a five-year bit.

My older brother, Pacho, was my heart. He was really the only father I had ever known since my own biological father had run out on my mother when I was just four years old. I had no love in my heart for him or any man who would do what he did to my mother. With my brother getting locked up, in a sense he was leaving, though when he had been home he always tried his best to provide for his child. At least that's what he told me. I didn't know because I was too busy trying to get my own life on track while surviving the rotten slums of the Bronx.

"Yo, Sammy, what's taking you so long, ma? You already knew I was coming over here. Bring my niece to me so I can make sure she good, then I'ma be on my way. Word up."

The big roach fell from the ceiling and smacked the table. Its legs kicked furiously, although it was trapped on its back.

The egg in its butt had been dislodged about an inch away from the roach. I blew at it to see if it would fly off of the table. It slid just a little way, so I blew some more until it hit the floor. Once there, it flipped onto its back and took off running under the refrigerator.

It seemed like as soon as it went under it, a big-ass rat stuck its head out from under the fridge. Its nose sniffed at the air, then it slowly made its way into the kitchen. It was the size of a one-month-old kitten, and just as hairy. Its red eyes searched for its next destination. I could hear its long claws dragging across the floor. It was enough to give me the heebie-jeebies.

I stomped my Airmax shoe at it, and it took off running under the stove. I jumped up out of my seat and took my chances standing in the living room. Even though I was born and bred in the Bronx, I was still not accustomed to rats and roaches, though a majority of my hood was. I was never able to settle for that being the norm for me. I wanted to reside in better living conditions. I didn't think my place was in the hood, so I never allowed myself to get comfortable, even though I came from a family that was deep within the belly of struggle. I wanted out, and I knew my exit was fast approaching.

Samantha came from the back room with a silk robe pulled tight around her voluptuous body. She was about five feet, five inches tall and weighed at least 150 pounds. She was brown-skinned with brown eyes and short, wavy hair that fell just below the back of her neck. She was 25 years old, like my older brother, and a resident of the Bronx River Houses. Or should I say the projects? She stayed on the tenth floor, and my mother stayed on the ninth.

She ran her fingers through her unkempt hair and licked her juicy lips with her eyes only partially opened. "Dang, Jahmani. Ain't nobody tell you to show up this early. I was still asleep. I had a long night." She yawned and stretched her arms over her head. She smelled like a hint of perfume with a trace of sex. I could tell she'd been getting down the night prior, either with herself or with a partner. Either way, it wasn't my business. I was there to make sure Lonnie was straight.

"Ma, it's eleven. You should have been up. When are you supposed to start back working?" I wiped the sweat from my forehead again. It was scorching in her pad. Sweat was running down my rib cage. I could literally feel it. "Why is it so hot in here?" I bombarded her with another question before she could answer the first one.

She took two more steps and sat on the arm of the couch, hunched over, and yawned into her fist again. The way she was positioned caused her robe to slide up her thighs a bit to the point I could clearly see she wasn't wearing panties or had any hair on her kitty.

"They done turned off my electricity. I was a few months behind, so my air conditioner ain't on. And I would have been going to work today, but I couldn't find no childcare for Lonnie. So until I do, I'm stuck. I'm down and out right now." She sighed.

Her bedroom door opened and Mikey, one of the familiar faces from the projects, walked out of it, looked into the living room where we were, and nodded his head in a 'what up?' fashion before heading into the bathroom and closing the door.

"Yo, so you got this nigga jumping up and down in between your thighs, but you can't get your electricity turned on? What type o' shit is that?" I asked, growing angry. I didn't feel like she should have been giving nobody no pussy if they couldn't help her better her situation. Any man would jump up and down inside of a woman all day long if she let him. Free pussy was the best pussy, but it was often the kind no one would respect. The harder a nigga had to work for the cat, the more he appreciated it. That was a fact. It pained me that she didn't know that truth. Made me sick to my stomach.

She frowned. "Here we go wit' this shit. Jahmani, I know you ain't bring yo' ass over here this early in the mornin' to get on my nerves? If so, I'll holler at you later. I ain't got time for this right now." She stood up and ran her hand over her face. There was a speck of cold in her eyes that she dug out. She grabbed a Kleenex and mugged me.

"Man, sit yo' ass down so we can finish this conversation. I don't know what type of dudes you been messing with since bro been gone, and that ain't my bidness, but you gon' respect me. Word up." I mugged her and sat on the couch myself.

She hesitated and looked like she wanted to defy my orders. She curled her lip and rolled her eyes before sitting across from me and crossing her thighs. The robe slid all the way back, revealing her whole left cheek. She clasped her fingers and looked everywhere but in my face. She was acting like a little-ass schoolgirl, and I wasn't feeling her immaturity. She was the mother of my niece, the first line of defense in this cold-ass world we lived in. If she didn't have her head together, then nine times out of ten my niece was headed for disaster. I had to nip that crap in the bud ahead of time.

"Yo, so tell me where you are with everything?" I said, trying to calm my temper. I saw Mikey walk past and back to her bedroom, and it pissed me off. That fool was known for being a bum and a stick-up kid. A low-life. He ain't have nothing going for himself. There was no way he should have been able to sleep under the same roof as my niece. None!

Samantha lowered her head. "What are you talking about, Jahmani?"

"The bills, Sammy. I need to know where you are with everything. What are you behind on?"

She shrugged her shoulders. "They cut my assistance because I lied about my job hours and income two months ago, so I'm basically messed up right now. I'm behind on all my bills. The lights, gas, food, my car note, clothes for Lonnie and myself. I have twenty dollars to my name, and that has to go into my gas-guzzling Neon. Then I have to get an oil change and my tires rotated. The brakes are going out as well, and your brother want me to put some money on the phone. I don't know what to do." She shook her head and brushed a roach off of the couch and stepped on it with her house shoe.

I nodded. I could tell she was defeated. She'd gotten pregnant with my niece young. Before she had, she'd already dropped out of high school, chasing behind my brother in the streets and treating his word as if it was God's. He'd caught her young, at the tender age of thirteen. Both of her parents had been heroin addicts before they overdosed and my brother took her under his wing for good.

In my opinion, I felt he did her a disservice. There is no telling where she would have been if she'd never chosen to follow behind a dope boy who had the game figured out in the slightest.

I had fifteen thousand dollars on me. Money I was going to use to re-up. I was in my second year of college on an athletic scholarship, majoring in sociology and minoring in criminal justice, which was ironic because I'd been in the slums doin' dirt ever since I was eleven years old.

I pulled a knot out of my pocket and licked my thumb, "How much is your rent per month?" I asked, looking over at her.

For the first time, she looked me in my face. She fidgeted on the couch and bucked her eyes. "Why, are you gon' help me wit' it?"

I was trying my best to not get frustrated. Mikey came out

of the bedroom and walked past us. He looked at all the money I was holding and bucked his eyes. He walked into the kitchen, got himself a glass of water, and headed back into the bedroom, closing the door behind him. I was so irritated I wanted to go in there and put his ass out. This punk was walking around her crib like he owned it. Wasn't paying not a bill in it, though. Man, that shit was annoying.

"Shorty, just answer my questions and let me handle everything else, a'ight? Stop answering my questions wit' a question. That's annoying me. Now go."

"I pay six hundred for rent. I'm one month behind and got four months left on my lease."

I counted out three gees and sat it on the table. "How much does the electric and gas come to for the rest of the year."

"Dang, you gon' pay it all the way up for the year?" Her eyes were as big as teacups. She opened her thighs wide, exposing her charms. I could see the crinkle of her sex lips.

"Samantha, close your legs, shorty. And what I just say about you asking me a question with one of my questions? Huh?"

"Dang, I'm sorry, Jahmani. It's just that it's unbelievable to me. Even when your brother was out here, he wasn't trying to pay none of my bills. So, for you to be is just mind boggling." She closed her thighs and crossed them, pulling the robe down as far as it could go.

"Let's get one thing straight. I ain't paying these bills for your benefit. I'm doing it for my niece, Lonnie. She don't deserve to be out on the street or sitting in a hot-ass house with no food. She is a princess. So, if I gotta step up to the plate because my brother can't right now, then so be it. So, what's the total?"

She closed her eyes. Her lips moved, but no sounds came out. When she opened her eyes, they were still looking up at the top of her head. "Um, if I was to be able to get ahead on everything, including the car and food, I would need at least ten thousand. That way I would be able to get Lonnie some school clothes, put some food in the house, get my car serviced, and all of the bills will be paid up for the year. I get my taxes in January, so I'll be able to handle things from there."

I licked my thumb again and counted out ten thousand dollars in all hundreds and fifties. I placed it in a neat stack on the table and looked across at her. "Sammy, this ten gees here. You should be able to take care of everything you need with this li'l paper so you can be ahead on everything. I don't like seeing you down and out, so you gotta get your shit together. You got a li'l girl looking up to you. Everything she see you doing, she gon' think it's okay for her to do when she get of age. We gotta break that cycle, do you understand me?"

She nodded. "I'm trying, Jahmani. I know it don't seem like it, but I really am trying to do and be better. It's just that I ain't never been on my own ever since I was born. I been following behind your bro since I was thirteen years old. During that whole time he sort of provided everything. That was until I got this crib. After that he sort of left me to figure things out on my own. Then he got knocked a year later, and it's been hard ever since then. I know I gotta do better, but I feel so lost."

I looked at her for a long time in sympathy. I could only guess what that feeling was like for her. It was no secret it was harder on our women than it was for us men. I mean, we could go out and get it by any means. But for a woman trying to survive in the unforgiving streets, it was nearly impossible. Especially factoring in their children, if they had any.

"Yeah, well, get your landlord on the phone, and we gon' sit here and pay every bill before I get up and go. I gotta make sure you're good before I leave here today, because it ain't no telling when I'm going to come holler at you again."

She scooted forward on the couch, pushing her robe backward and opened her thighs, flashing her treasures again before she stood. "Just wait right here. I'ma go and get my phone. All of the information I'll need is right there inside of it. Please don't leave," she begged and rushed to her bedroom.

I popped my shirt. I was so damn hot I couldn't think straight. I adjusted my pistol on my hip. The sweat was making the steel feel itchy. I took it off of my waist and tucked it into the crease of the couch right under the arm.

Lonnie's bedroom door opened. She stood in it for a second, rubbing her eyes. She had a teddy bear in her hand, its arm dragging across the floor. "Uncle?" she whispered.

I turned toward her and held my arms out. "Come here, baby! You okay?" I couldn't wait to feel her in my arms. Lonnie was my heart and had been ever since she'd come out of the womb. The mole on her left cheek was reminiscent of the one I had on my left cheek. She also had curly hair, like myself, though I kept mine cut real short in a Mohawk-like style. We were both light caramel, as well. My brother Pacho had often joked about Lonnie actually being my daughter, but I'd never laid a finger on Samantha. The thought had never crossed my mind. I didn't care how bad she was.

Lonnie ran across the floor and into my arms. "Uncle. I missed you so much. Can I go with you, because it's too hot in this house?" I noticed there were traces of sweat around the edges of her hair and a clear path of it along her right temple. I wiped this away with my thumb. "Please take me with you. I'll be good. I promise I will."

"Oh, so that's the only reason you want to go with me?" I teased, kissing her little hot cheek and hugging her to my chest.

"No. I just don't want to be here anymore. I don't like it here. There is a mouse in my room. And I'm scared of it." She wrapped her arms around my neck and melted my heart in the process.

I closed my eyes and smiled. "Aw, baby. I wish I could take you with me, but I got so much work to do. I'll tell you what, how about you come and spend a night with me this weekend? How I does that sound?" I kissed her cheek again.

She shook her head. "I want to come today. It's too hot in this house. My mama make me stay in the room too much. I want to go outside and play. I want to go with you, Uncle. Don't you love me anymore?"

She looked up at me with her big brown eyes. Man, that had me feeling so damn weak. I loved and hated when she gave me those eyes. I couldn't turn her down. How could I? She was my heart. "Okay, baby. Let me ask your mother if it's okay for you to go with me, and if she says it's cool, I'll take you with me for a couple of days. That sound good?"

She kissed my cheek and hugged my neck so tight I knew she was happy. It warmed my heart. Lonnie was everything to me.

Samantha came out of her bedroom and slammed the door. She had an angry look on her face. The noise caused Lonnie to jump off of my lap and stand up, frightened. I could literally see her shaking as if she was freezing cold.

Samantha stopped in place and mugged her. "What are you doing out of the room?" she asked her, sounding impatient.

Before Lonnie could answer, I got offended and stood up. "Wait a minute. Don't be coming at her like that. I called her in here so I could get me some hugs and kisses. She was the reason I came over here to begin with. Did you forget?"

Samantha's face softened. "Oh, I didn't know. I just don't like her in grown men's faces. That's all. Baby, go back to your room until me and your uncle is finished talking. Okay?" She pointed. "Go on."

Lonnie inched her way over to me and grabbed my hand, looking out at her mother as if she was expecting her to go ballistic. Lonnie looked up at me. "Can you ask her, Uncle? Please?" she asked, letting my hand go and walking across the carpet slowly.

"I'm taking her wit' me for a few days. You can do whatever you want to do while she gone, but she coming wit' me. I'ma take her shopping and spend some time wit' her. That's my heart."

Samantha shrugged her shoulders. "Shid, I don't care if you do. I need a break. Just bring her back Sunday night." She sat on the couch and crossed her thighs again. "Let's handle this business real fast before you change your mind."

"Baby, you're going wit' me, so just chill in your room a li'l while longer, and then we'll be leaving soon. I promise." I watched her smile and run into her room. I took my seat back on the couch across from Samantha. "Awright, let's get all this shit taken care of so I can spoil her."

She nodded. "So, we'll pay up the rent first, right?" She started to dial a number on her cell phone. "The landlord is in the building already. I was just talking to him on the phone. Let me tell him to swing down here." She held the phone to her ear and smiled at me.

I was getting more and more sweaty. I was ready to take Lonni and bounce. I'd seen more than one rat, and roaches everywhere. I didn't know how much more itching I could take.

Chapter 2

Samantha's bedroom door opened and Mikey stepped out with a blue bandana around his face and a .38 Special in is right hand. He stepped into the living room and pointed the gun at me. "Nigga, you already know what time it is. Break yo' muthafucking self. I need all of that paper!"

Samantha dropped her phone to the floor and screamed. "What are you doing, Mikey? What are you doing? That's my baby da brother," she cried, then held her hands up in the air.

He rushed over to her and slapped her across the face with the pistol. It split her skin. She fell off of the couch holding her face. Blood gushed through her fingers.

"Fuck Pacho! Bitch, I don't care about him, you, or this nigga. I gotta get mines. Word is bond." He kicked her in the side, flippin' her over, then aimed his gun at me again. "Nigga, break yo'self."

I mugged this lowlife-ass nigga. "Son, the money right there on the table. Right here You want it, go ahead and take it. It's all I got." I knew he had to hear I was in here trying to help her pay her bills. For him to come out and do what he was doing meant he was a lowlife in every sense of the word.

He nodded his head. "Yeah, son, just stay yo' punk-ass right here and it won't be nothing. I'ma take this li'l bread and be on my way. Y'all better act like this shit never happened. That's all I can say. You don't want it wit' my Crip niggas, cuz. Word is bond, we wipe out whole generations, kid. Lay on yo' stomach."

I scrunched my face. "Nigga, I don't give a fuck what you 'bout, I ain't moving. Just take that li'l chump change and be on yo' way. Shit ain't gotta go no further than this. I can take this loss on the chin. It is what it is."

"What, nigga?" He kicked Samantha in the ribs so hard he

knocked the wind out of her. She lay on her back with her eyes closed, struggling to breathe. "Nigga, I said get yo' punk-ass on yo' stomach or else I'ma put two holes in yo' shit. What it gon' be?" He stepped closer to where I was seated, cocking the hammer on his .38.

I held my hands on each side of my face. "A'ight, just chill, nigga, damn." I slowly eased from the couch down to my knee. Once there, I put my arms out in a push-up position and lowered myself to the ground. I wasn't feelin this cat. I was searching for any opening to attack his ass. I wasn't worried about him killing me. If that happened, it happened. I knew my death date was already written in God's book, so if today was that day, then I was ready to roll wit' it.

Mikey placed his shoe on my back and raised it, then stomped me so hard right in the center that I felt a tingle go down my legs. "Bitch-ass nigga! Next time I tell you to do something, you do it right away. You got that, kid?" he spat with saliva flying out of his mouth.

I was too busy trying to catch my breath to respond. I felt like I'd been shot in my lung or something. Roaches crawled all around me, and I was certain the same rat from before ran across my face and under the couch, wiggling its body to squeeze all the way under it. "Fuck you, nigga," was all I managed to get out, but I was so hoarse I was unsure if he'd heard me or not. My rib felt like it was broken.

He knelt down and patted my pockets, sticking his hand in a out of them as if he was a professional. He took the remaining five thousand that wasn't on the table and tucked it into his pocket. "My nigga, I knew you was holding out. Trying to pay this ratchet-ass bitch's bills. You done lost yo' fucking mind." He stood up and pulled a pillowcase out of his underwear, popped it out, and filled it with the money from the table. "Take that watch off, too, and that link. I gotta have all that shit."

Even though it hurt me to move in the slightest, I managed to get the jewelry off of my neck. I tossed it at his feet. "Huh, nigga, take that shit and get the fuck out of here. You ain't got shit else to prove." I groaned, feeling my ribs ache.

He picked it up and kicked me in the side like he'd done Samantha. I rolled onto my other side and squeezed my eyes tightly together. I couldn't breathe for a few seconds, and my heart was pounding in my chest. My eyes were Iowan hazy. I'd never been more vexed in my entire life.

Mikey grabbed all of the money and jewelry, then made his way back into the bedroom. For what, I have no clue. I could hear him rummaging around the room.

Lonnie's bedroom door opened. She stood in the middle of it with tears running down her cheeks. "Uncle! Uncle!" She dropped her teddy bear and held her arms out for me, stomping her little feet in place. She looked to her mother's bedroom and broke into a fit of coughs. "Uncle!"

I struggled to come to my knees, the pain in my ribs throbbing so bad I couldn't breathe without wincing in pain. On the floor across from me, Samantha curled into a ball with blood running out of her nose. "Help me. Help me. Somebody, Please."

I rolled onto my butt and struggled to stand, then held my arms out for Lonnie to see it was cool to come to me.

She opened her eyes wide and made a step forward when Mikey came out Samantha's room with the gun in his hand. He rushed forward and grabbed a handful of her hair. "Bitch, didn't your mama tell you to stay yo' li'l ass in the room?" He flung her against the wall and kicked her in the side before slamming her door closed. I could hear her groaning and crying at the top of her lungs, and that crushed my soul. I felt like I'd failed to protect my little angel.

Mikey came out of the hallway with the gun in his hand. "She be alright. Lay yo' punk-ass back down, nigga, 'fore I cap you."

I slid back down to my stomach, but scooted as close to the couch as I could get. It rested against my right shoulder. My face was close to a pack of roaches that ran all over the place as I settled. I didn't give a fuck what took place. I saw I was going to have to kill this nigga. He had taken thing way too far. I could have accepted the robbery aspect of it, but now he had put his hands on my niece and her mother. That meant he had to die. I was a Bronx kid. We didn't accept that level of disrespect. Mikey should have known that.

Mikey moved into the kitchen and opened the cupboard. I don't know what he did from there because I couldn't see. I could only hear him. When he came back into the living room, his pillowcase looked like it had been filled with canned goods. Another sign he was a trifling-ass nigga. What type of man would steal the little food a woman had to provide for her daughter? Son was mad grimy and had to reap what he sowed.

He came back out of the kitchen, dropped his pillowcase by the door, and made his way across the carpet toward Samantha's face. "Bitch, who was you talking to?" He rolled her over as he grabbed the phone from the side of her, and looked at it. He moved her arms from in front of her face. "Bitch, did you hear what I said?" The blue rag had fallen off of his face. He grabbed her by the throat and squeezed. "Answer me!"

She kicked her legs wildly, her short robe sailing open. He slapped her across the face twice and continued to choke her. Every time she kicked, she exposed her secret places.

I don't know how or where I got the strength from, but some way I lunged from the carpet and tackled his bitch-ass. We wound up on top of Samantha. I cocked my head back and slammed it into his face while my hands took ahold of the pistol. He hit at my back so hard I bit my tongue. I kept my arms around him, and he held just as firm. Blood spilled out of his nose and mouth He was way more stringy than I imagined.

"Bitch-ass nigga! You wanna pick on these females?" *Bam*! Another head-butt knocked him backward. He kicked his feet, knocking the gun right out of my hands. It slid across the carpet and wound up against the wall just before the entrance to the kitchen.

He jumped up with blood leaking from his face and made a dash for it. I tackled his ass against the wall, picked him up, and slammed him onto his back so hard I heard it crunch. "Ahh!" he groaned with his eyes closed, then shocked the shit out of me when he jumped up and threw up his guards. He rushed me, swinging haymakers. Before I had time to block his first one, it caught me on the chin and knocked me backward. His second blow smashed my jaw, and I got so dizzy all I could see were stars.

"Nigga, let's get it on, cuz!"

I flew into the wall, then rushed him, swinging at the air. It seemed like it was two of him. I was messed up and praying he didn't go for the gun. If he had, he would've had me dead to rights.

But, lucky for me, he wasn't that smart. He rushed me, bear-hugged me, and slammed me on my back, though. I clasped my fingers in his shirt and head-butted him again, this time as hard as I could. I literally heard his nose snap.

"Aw! Aw! Aw! My fucking nose! My fucking nose!" He jumped up and ran, placing his back on the wall. Blood dripped down his wrists as he held his hands together over his nose protectively.

I looked to move in to capitalize off of his injury. As soon as I took two steps, he dropped to the floor and dove toward the gun, his fingers just grazing the handle.

I ran as fast as I could, still dizzy, and kicked the gun into the kitchen, then stomped in on the side of his jaw and kicked him directly in the face. I could feel the point of my toe sink into his flesh. He threw his hands into the air, and rolled against the wall, holding his face in his hands, groaning into them loudly.

"Sammy, take yo' ass in that room and get my niece out of here," I snapped at Samantha. My ribs were killing me. I wrapped my arm around them as I watched Mikey rise to his feet and grab a steak knife out of the drawer in her kitchen. He removed his hand from his face. Blood spilled down his neck, drenching is shirt.

"Bitch-ass nigga, I'm finna kill you. I'm finna kill you, nigga. That's on gang, cuz." He held the knife up and made his way toward me.

I backed away and looked around for something to grab. Roaches were all over the floor. By his foot, two big rats scurried from under the stove and ran along the wall behind him. They stopped about five feet away from me and stood on their hind legs. I didn't notice until right then one of them had a smaller one up under it that must've been its baby.

"Bruh, just get yo' ass out shorty crib. You ain't robbing nobody in here. Take yo' dope fien' somewhere else, kid," I said, still looking around for a weapon of some sort.

"Jahmani!" Samantha shouted. When I looked in her direction, she was taking my gun out of the cushion of her couch and tossin' it to me. As soon as I grabbed it, Mikey rushed me and stabbed me in the right shoulder. He jerked the blade out and slammed it into my chest. Then he took a step back, nodding his head.

When I looked down and saw the handle sticking out of

me, I damn near freaked out. My eyes got big as saucers. I raised the gun and cocked it By the time I aimed it at him, he tackled me to the wall. The back of my head slammed into it so hard I grew dizzy. But I was already in fight-for-my-life mode.

He punched me across the jaw. "You trying to kill me, nigga? I ain't going out like a bitch!" Another punch across my cheek made my eyes water.

"Get the fuck off of me," I groaned, feeling like I couldn't breathe. With the knife lodged inside of me, it felt like somebody overweight was sitting on my chest. It was so painful I was shaking.

I kneed him in the nuts, causing him to fly backward and off of me. As soon as he gave me about a foot to raise my arm, I raised it and grabbed the back of his neck. Placing the barrel of my gun into his stomach, I let off three shots. *Boom. Boom. Boom.* Two ripped through his stomach and came out of his back, slamming into the ceiling. The third one didn't exit at all.

He staggered backward and fell against the stove, holding his stomach. Blood gushed out of his holes. He opened his mouth, but no words came out. His eyes slowly rolled to the back of his head, then his body went limp.

I struggled to get to my feet, the knife still lodged deep in my chest. The smoking gun in my hand felt as if it weighed a thousand pounds. I couldn't believe I had just killed him. I had just taken a life. Fuck. They would put me in prison for the rest of my life. I would never see the streets again. *Aw, hell nall.* This couldn't be.

Samantha came out of the living room and stood in the doorway of the kitchen. She covered her mouth with her hand and shook her head. "Oh my God, Jahmani. Oh my God! What did you do?"

I pointed toward the living room. "Shut up," I wheezed. "Stay yo' ass in there. Don't let my niece see this shit." I struggled to breathe. Every time I took a breath, it felt like the knife was sliding deeper into my chest.

"What's that sticking out of you? Oh my God! You're stabbed!" She rushed to my side and wrapped her arm around my neck. Her hand went around the handle of the knife, ready to pull it out of me. "I got you, Jahmani. I got you." She wrapped her fingers around it and tensed up.

"No!" I croaked and fell into a fit of harsh coughing. She jumped backward with her hands in the air. "Don't pull it out. You pull that shit out and it's gon' kill me!" I fell against the wall and slid down it. My mouth felt dry, like I'd eaten a handful of sand. Roaches crawled around my hand that landed on the ground. "You gotta help me get rid of this nigga's body. Then get me to the hospital. I can't go down for this shit. You keep your mouth closed and I'll pay all of your bills for as long as I got air in my lungs. Do you hear me? It's fifteen thousand in there right now. Fourteen of it is yours. Just leave me a gee and my jewelry. A'ight?" I smacked my lips and closed my eyes for a second. I was losing my strength, but I knew I needed to get up. I had to get rid of Mikey's body. There was no way I was prepared to go down for his murder. Even though it was self-defense, the state of New York would surely make it seem as if our scuffle was gang related. I wasn't fit to do life in nobody's prison.

Samantha fell to her knees beside me and kissed my cheek. "I ain't no snitch, Jahmani. I ain't gon' say shit. Just tell me what you want me to do." She stood up and looked over at the corpse of Mikey. A pool of blood had formed around him. The kitchen floor was getting more and more flooded with his fluids.

"Go and get me two blankets. The thicker the better. I'ma

wrap this nigga up and throw him in the dumpster. Go!"

I watched her run off. I struggled to get back to my feet, feeling like there was ice in my lungs. With each step I took, the blade of the knife lodged itself deeper. I was cursing myself for not allowing Samantha to remove it. I was sure I was causing more damage to my body.

I made my way over to him, grabbed his arm, and pulled him across the kitchen floor. His blood made it easier for me to complete the task. Once he was in the middle of the floor, I laid him out the long way and waited for Samantha to return with the blankets. She came three minutes later and dropped them beside me. It took me five full minutes to get him wrapped the way I needed him to be. Once he was, I scooted away from him on my ass. "Go make sure ain't nobody in the hallway. Hurry up."

Samantha stuck her head out of the door and looked both ways. Then she stepped into the hall and disappeared.

I closed my eyes. I was getting sleepy. I felt if I could take a little nap, then I would be good to go. I just needed to rest my mind for a few.

Before I knew it, I'd drifted off. I awoke moments later. My chest was really throbbing. I felt like my insides were being carved out of me. Tears flooded down my cheeks.

Samantha was dragging Mikey's wrapped body cross the kitchen floor, struggling to do so. I forced myself up and grabbed his legs in my hands. "Grab the top portion, and let's get a move on."

She nodded and picked up the top portion of his body. "I got you, Jahmani. I swear on my daughter, I got you. I know this only happened because you were protecting me and Lonnie. I ain't gon' let you go down for this shit," she cried.

I was blacking in and out of consciousness for a second at a time, but somehow, someway, we made it to the boiler room.

Ghost

When we got there, Samantha helped me to hoist Mikey up and into the incinerator. We forced his body all the way inside of it before I collapsed and fell on my back.

***

When I opened my eyes the next time, an IV was being hooked up to my arm, and I was being rushed into surgery. The doctors and nurses seemed to be in a frenzy. I felt higher than I had ever been before. I closed my eyes and fell back to sleep.

I could hear the doctors' voices as they worked on me. I could feel them poking and prodding, hear the sounds of the machines as they fought to help me stay alive. The pain in my chest felt worse than it had earlier.

Visions of Mikey's dead body lying on the kitchen floor haunted me. In my dreams he hollered out in pain and covered his stomach, asking me why. Why did I take his life? How could I?

Then his face became distorted. It melted, and suddenly so did his entire body. It melted down into a pile of alley rats. They ran every which way and disappeared

Chapter 3

Two Months Later

I didn't care about or love nobody in this world a much as I loved my mother, Inez. She was Puerto Rican and black with beautiful brown eyes and golden-colored skin. She was only 4'11" tall with naturally curly hair and a fiery personality. She was the type who would tell you exactly what was on her mind and wouldn't give a care what you thought about it. She was a strong woman with only one weakness: my mother suffered from epilepsy. She had seizures that would come out of nowhere, and they made it hard for her to maintain employment. She also had to have a caregiver come and watch over her for five hours a day.

About two months after I'd killed Mikey, and three weeks after I'd been cleared to leave the hospital, I was missing her and thought I'd pay her a visit. She stayed on the ninth floor of the Bronx River Houses projects, the same building Samantha and Lonnie stayed in.

After we'd forced Mikey's body into the incinerator, instead of it burning him up and getting rid of the body, the fire had only managed to burn for about twenty minutes after we threw him in there, then it went out. To make a long story short, his body was discovered partially burned two days later by the superintendent of the building and reported to the local authorities. This put the building on lockdown and the entire police force on high alert around the area.

When my mother opened the door to her apartment, she looked as if she were just waking up. Her long curly hair was everywhere. She wore a long gown with a robe over it. The scent from her apartment was all marijuana. I knew that all of her weed was imported from San Juan, Puerto Rico. It was always the best of the best.

She had a tightly-rolled joint in her left hand with smoke coming from it. "Step in, son. I don't want none of them damn police looking in my house. They been all over this flight all morning, knocking on people doors, asking about that damn lowlife they found in the boiler room. Close my door." She walked away from me, still mumbling to herself.

I stepped in and closed her door behind me. The apartment was dark. The only light was from the seven candles burning to illuminate the picture of the Virgin Mary that hung on her mantel in the living room. "Mama, wasn't the rent due, like, two day ago? And if so, why didn't you call me?" I asked, following her into her bedroom, where she hopped on her bed after taking her house shoes off.

She puffed on her joint, tapping its body, dumping the ashes into the ashtray. "Son, before you come over here worrying about me, why don't you tell me how you're doing? How is your chest doing? Let Mama see," she demanded. She got on her knees and made her way across the bed, grabbing the hem of my shirt before I could grab it myself. She pulled it upward, exposing my wife beater underneath. Then she pulled that out of my pants and upward as well. I helped her pull it off and dropped my shirts on her bed.

She took her fingers and ran them lightly over the patch that still covered the wound on my chest, then ran her fingers over the ones in my shoulder. "You gon' tell me how you did this, boy? What happened to you? I wanna know right now," she demanded, holding my face in her hands.

I shook my head and backed up. "For as long as I been alive, I have never lied to you. I don't want to start today. Just know that my wounds are healing, and I'm good." I kissed her on the cheek and hugged her. "Now, what's good with the rent? The Super show up yet?" I asked, trying my best to change the subject.

She waved me off. "Don't worry about the Super. Mardi is on her way over here. She says she misses you, and she wants to make things right. I think you should hear her out. I got a good feeling about you two this time." She smiled and sat on the bed, looking up at me with her eyes beaming.

"Ma, I already told you I ain't messing with her no more. I ain't never finna allow no other female to get as close to me as she did. That's the first female I ever trusted, and last. If it ain't you, I ain't going."

I sat on the chair across from her bed and pulled out a knot of hundreds totaling three thousand dollars. It was all I had to my name, but I had to pay my mother's bills. I already knew what time it was. Every month it came down to me handling my business for her, and she always tried to brush it off as if it didn't need to be done. My mother was a proud woman, raised by her father's side of the family, which was full-blooded Puerto Rican. My grandfather was a very proud man even though he struggled his entire life to make ends meet. My mother said she'd never known her father to accept or take any handouts from anybody. She said if he couldn't go out and work for it himself, then he'd rather go without. I was that same kind of person, so I understood.

I handed her seven $100 bills. "Huh, Mama, this is six hundred for the rent and an additional hundred for you to put into your pocket. Just in case you need anything."

Instead of taking the money, she grabbed a pillow from her bed and hugged it. "Baby, why won't you give Mardi another chance? She's the only girl here in New York that is from my village. Everybody makes mistakes. Will you hold this over her head forever?" she asked, not paying attention to the money I dropped directly in front of her.

I slid my shirts back. "Real women know how to hold their man down, Mama. They don't cheat just because they're out of the country and back on the island. She was the first female I had ever been with who I never cheated on. But ever since then my head been screwed up. Now its all about me getting what I need out of a woman, and I keep it moving. I ain't got no time for relationships. I'm trying to buy you a house and make my way through college so I can finally pull us out of this ghetto death grip. If I can't make it happen, then who will?"

I leaned over and hugged her, kissed her lips, and stood up, tucking my beater into my pants and dusting myself off. I was one of those real particular dudes when it came to dressing and my appearance as a whole. I liked to stay sharp, my clothes fresh and designer. My hair had to stay cut and freshly edged at all times. I'd been that way ever since my first day of kindergarten. Even though we never had much, I felt as long as I kept my outside looking like we did, people would never know the truth. So I did what I had to do to keep myself presentable.

My mother climbed out of the bed and stood in front of me. "Baby, you know I am thankful for everything you do for me, right? You do understand that after all of these years, it is still painful for me to sit back and allow for you to take care of me. You, my youngest son, to whom I should be caring for? You understand the heartache that comes along with that?"

I wrapped my arms around her little body, and held her to me, kissing her forehead. "Mama, my job is to make sure you're always taken care of. I can't do much right now, but in time I'ma get you out of these Projects and into your own home. A nice one, too. Like one of them joints out in Queens where you can have your own li'l backyard. You can plant you some vegetables like shorty did on that movie, *Baby Boy*. You'll love that. Put a piece of Puerto Rico in there and everything. Wouldn't you love that?" I looked down at her.

She had her eyes closed, smiling. "Aw, baby, that sounds so good. I know you're going to make it happen. I just can't wait. I feel like these projects are going to be the death of me ever since they found that fool shot up and burned in the boiler room. The Bloods and Crips have been at each other's throats worse than ever. They think one of the Bloods killed in retaliation for another killing that happened three days prior to his. That boy was shot up and sat on fire by the Crips. Do you remember hearing about that?"

I shrugged my shoulders. "Very vaguely. You know I stay in my own lane. I don't be trying to hear about what's going on in this hood because you won't be here for much longer. I gotta make it happen for you, Mama. I just have to." I hugged her tighter and exhaled. I would go nuts if something happened to my mother before I could move her out of the Projects. Sometimes I thought about how my father had left her to fend for herself while raising his kids, and I wanted to snap. What type of man got down like that? I didn't get it.

She took a step back and looked up at me. "Baby, it's the first Sunday of the month next week. You know what that means, right?

I lowered my head. "Yes, ma'am, I do."

"Well good, because I want you to spend the whole day in church with me. That's our agreement. You give me one Sunday a month, I'll pray over you all that day, then you can go back to your sinful life," she giggled.

There was a knock at the door that caused her to jump. "Lord, please don't let it be them dang ol' police. I don't feel like dealing with them today. They didn't investigate the buildings this much when Fred Hampton got choked out by the damn police. Stay in here, baby. I don't need them all in your face, either." She left the bedroom and closed the door.

As soon as she was out, I rushed to her purse and opened

it, went right to where she normally kept her money, and peeked inside of it. I saw there was about five dollars in singles and a bunch of pennies. That crushed my heart. I stuffed a hundred dollar bill inside of it and closed it back. Next I pulled out the top drawer of her dresser to see how much weed she had left. I discovered about a dime bag full. I knew I would have to get her some more because along with the seizures, my mother suffered from severe migraines. The weed helped to suppress them. I didn't like her being in pain at all. It was like I could feel whenever she was hurting.

I closed the drawer and flicked the lights in the room on and off to make sure they were still on and hadn't been turned off. It wasn't that I suspected my mother of being irresponsible, it was just that she never liked asking for help. I couldn't remember if I'd already paid the light bill or not, so I had to make sure.

After confirming the electricity was still on, I turned the lights back off and sat on the edge of her bed. My cheat throbbed. I had to get home to my pain medication.

There was a knock on the door, and then the knob twisted and the door came inward. "Baby, somebody here wants to talk to you." She lowered her voice. "Please give her a chance for me." She blew me a kiss and moved out of the way.

Mardi stepped past her in all of her 5'6" of glory. Though she was full-blooded Puerto Rican, her skin was dark like she'd been born in Africa. Her eyes were gray, her hair curly and long. It flowed down her back, kissing her waistline. She weighed about 130 pounds and had breasts that filled a D cup. Her waist was slim, but everything else below it radiated sex. It was hard to look into her pretty eyes because her body was so immaculate and well put together.

She'd been my first girlfriend, dating all the way back to our second grade year. I remembered beating up a bunch of boys my age over her, whooping them at recess because I was so jealous. I didn't like boys talking to her or putting their dirty hands on my girl. I had that possessive trait, and she was just as bad. As many fights as I got into with boys over her, she'd gotten into that many with girls over me.

I stood up and ran my hand over my face. "Mardi. Damn, ma, what you doing here?" I asked, feeling some type of way. Even though I was angry at her for cheating on me a few years back, every time this woman came into my presence, I felt emotionally sick. Like we were still connected and I was fighting the process.

She flipped on the lights. I saw she was dressed in a tight-fitting blue and gray Fendi dress that had her curves looking right. The hem of the dress stopped just above her knees. Her pretty feet were encased inside some matching red bottoms. She smelled if Fendi perfume, the diamond studs in her ear causing her eyes to pop. Her curly hair was pulled back into a long, bushy ponytail. The edges were wavy. She looked good.

"Damn, *papi*, it's crazy how your mother has to basically trap you just so I can talk to you. Don't our past mean anything to you at all?" she asked, stepping in front of me, opening her arms, and wrapping them around me. She laid her head on my chest and exhaled as if her mission was accomplished.

I hugged her for a second and felt old feelings coming back. I had to get her up off of me. This was my first love. There was way too much history and chemistry there. In addition to being my first love, she'd been the first girl to give me that kitty. That butt, too, but that was years later.

I released her, stepped to the side, and ran my hand over my curly mohawk. I had six inches and about fifty pounds on her. "Yo, it really ain't no reason for us to be hollering, shorty. I'm trying to perfect so much stuff in my life that I ain't got time for the drama. You did what you did, and that's that. I ain't got nothing else to really say other than I wish you the best, and I'll always love you. I just can't be with you no more."

She sighed and lowered her head. "Damn, so you gon' hold one mistake over my head forever? After all we been through?"

"I ain't holding nothing over your head. I forgive you. I just want better for myself. I gave you a chance, and you failed. Life goes on. 'Nah mean?" I finished, getting myself together. I had to get up out of there. Her perfume was killing me. My dick was getting hard and everything. It looked like she'd gotten thicker, and Mardi had always had some snapper down below. Her kitty was good. The feel and the taste, man I wanted to taste it bad. I had to get out of that room. I grabbed the door knob and twisted it. "I'll see you around, though."

She grabbed me aggressively and pulled me back. "You not about to walk out on me, Jahmani. I don't give a fuck what I did. You gon' respect me enough to hear me out. I gave you a lotta years of my life. Now, don't do me like this," she said through clenched teeth.

I yanked my arm out of her grasp, and turned to face her. "Shorty, you already know I don't like nobody grabbing all on me. You can get your point across without touching me and shit." My heart was beating fast, and that wasn't good because although I was only twenty years old, I had high blood pressure. It was inherited. It didn't take much for my blood pressure to get way up there. It caused me to have a short temper, and I'd often get dizzy quick. I stressed and worried a lot because I was always trying to figure out difficult tasks, things that would place myself and my family in a better position all across the board.

Mardi turned her back to me and covered her face with her hands, then began to sob. "Why are you doing me like this,

Jahmani? You know how much I love you. You know I would never do anything to hurt you. You're my everything. Damn, this ain't fair." She fell to her knees and broke into tears, sobbing loudly, rocking back and forth.

I felt like shit. I didn't like making a female I honestly cared about cry. I just hated to see it. So I fell to my knees beside her and wrapped my arms around her body. "Mami, it ain't that serious. I ain't trying to hurt you, and I still love you, too. I'm just not trying to go there no more. You fucked up, Mardi. We supposed to have meant more to each other."

She broke down even harder in my arms, saying words I could not understand. Her body shivered. She held me tighter, her face landing in the crux of my neck.

There was a knock on the door, and then my mother stuck her face inside the room. "I'm sorry, babies. But Mardi, you need to tell him the truth. Tell him what really happened in San Juan," my mother urged. "Go on, baby. You say you love him."

Mardi shook her head. "It's not going to make things any better. He hates me now. Just look at how he acts toward me," she cried.

I cocked my neck back and looked her over. "Mardi, what is she talking about?" I asked, confused and a little irritated. Me and my mother rarely kept things from each other. The fact she knew something about Mardi that I did not was making me angry, especially if it was something that could potentially affect the way I viewed her.

"It's nothing, Jahmani. Just let me go." She jumped to her feet and ran out of the apartment, slamming the door. I could hear her whimpering in the hallway while she ran down it in tears.

My mother walked over to me and smacked me on the back of the head. "Go get that girl! Now, Jahmani, or I swear

I'm gon' do the best I can to whoop your muscle-bound ass. That girl didn't cheat on you. Her dumbass girlfriend put something in her drink, then the girl and her boyfriend took advantage of Mardi while she was fucked up. So, you see, it wasn't her fault. That girl love you more than any other female ever will. I believe that."

I stayed there on my knees, dumbfounded, for what felt like ten full minutes before I got up, kissed my mother, and ran off in pursuit of Mardi with a heavy heart.

Chapter 4

I rang the doorbell for the fourth time. Finally, Mardi stepped to the door and stuck her eye into the peephole.

"What do you want, Jahmani? I don't feel like talking right now," she said with her voice breaking up. "I can't take what you're putting me through. I have a photo shoot in the morning. I need to have myself well put together. That goes for my mental as well."

I was standing in the hallway of the walk-up building she stayed in. Her apartment was on the seventh floor. I was already winded and hot. The hallway felt like it was a thousand degrees. "Yo, open the door, goddess. I need to holler at you. I ain't trying to do this shit out here in this hot-ass hallway." I wiped the sweat from my forehead and frowned at the peephole. I knew she was watching me, and that made me even more irritated. I beat on the door again. "Open up, Mardi!"

The door opened directly across from hers, and an old woman about the age of seventy stuck her head out of it yelling in Spanish, "Stop making all of that noise! She's not the only resident in the building! Respect me or I'm going to call the police and have the both of you deported." I was able to translate it, speaking Spanish fluently thanks to my mother's parents.

Mardi finally unlocked the door and pulled me in. "I'm sorry, Mrs. Flores, it'll never happen again. Please forgive his ill manners. No home training," she smiled and looked up at me.

The old woman slammed her door in response. "These kids these days. Santa Maria, help me!" she hollered in Spanish.

Mardi closed the door and sighed. "What do you want, Jahmani? I thought you didn't have anything else to say to me?" She walked away and headed toward her front room. She'd changed into a tight, gray pair of boy shorts that looked a tad too small for her and a matching tank top that showed off her flat stomach and belly ring. Her bare feet dug into the carpet as she walked. Her cheeks jiggling with every step, along with her thighs.

"Yo, why you didn't tell me what really happened down there? Had you did that, we'd still be together." I made my way into the front room. I looked around her apartment. It looked nice and cozy. She had a three-piece furniture set, a big screened television planted on the wall, and her kitchen, and front rooms were nice and neat. It smelled of incense. There were pictures of Saint Mary and Jesus hanging all over the apartment.

She turned around and pointed at me. "You should have forgiven me, or at least dug deeper to find out how I could ever cheat on you to begin with. We've been through way too much together. You should have known I could never do that."

I didn't feel like arguing with her about who was right, or how things should have went. The bottom line was she had not cheated, which meant I was free to lust after that body again. Her boy shorts were all up in her gap. They'd molded to her kitty print. I could make out both sex lips. She didn't have a bra on under her tank top, either. Her areolas were apparent. The nipples stuck up through the material. The sight was enough to drive me crazy.

She took a seat on the couch, and I slid down beside her. "Yo, I don't want to get into all that right now. All I can say is I'm sorry, and we should have gotten more of an understanding. You gained some weight?" I asked, sucking my bottom lip. Her thighs looked real juicy.

She jumped up in a panic. "What, you think I'm getting fat? Oh shit, I hope not."

She made a move to rush out of the front room, I guessed to look at herself in the mirror. I grabbed her wrist, stopping her. "Hold fast, goddess. I ain't saying it like that. I'm saying you looking good as hell. It look like your body is filling out lovely."

I pulled her in front of me and placed my hands on her ass cheeks. The bottoms of them were sticking out of the panties. They were dark and lovely, like the perm. I squeezed them and pulled her forward. At the same time I scooted forward on the couch until her crotch was inches away from my face. I took my nose and sniffed the front of her panties, then kissed them, licking the material.

She closed her eyes. "I'm still mad at you, Jahmani. You're not just about to come in here and get you some. We need to talk about our split. I'm emotionally hurting right now."

"I know, baby. I am, too. We gon' get to the bottom of all of that. I promise." I pulled the material of the panties into her lips, then sucked at the flesh of her labia that was exposed to my sight. I sucked first the right lip into my mouth, then the left one. They were hairless, hot, and slippery.

She shook. "Don't do this right now, Jahmani. You ain't touched me in so long. I'm so confused. Please, just stop. I'm begging you."

I pulled her panties all the way to the side and swiped my tongue up and down her gap as if it was a credit card. Her lips fell on each side of my tongue, trapping it. Then I pulled it out and kissed her right on her opening. Her juices ran out of her and onto my tongue. I gripped her ass cheeks and brought her crotch to my face. Now I was slurping and sucking like my life depended on it. The scent of her pussy wafted up my nose and into my brain. My dick throbbed in my Gucci boxers, worming its way out along my waistline, the head already wet

39

with precum. "I missed this taste, baby. I missed this right here. Open these lips up." I yanked her panties down and around her thighs. "Hold them feet apart."

She spaced her feet and kept her thighs apart. Her li'l cat was swollen, oozing its cream down her thick thighs. It looked as if she was slowly peeing. "Please don't do this, Jahmani."

I took my tongue and ran it from the inside of her right knee all the way up to her cat, covered her whole pussy with my mouth, and swiped my tongue back and forth in between her lips before licking back down her other thigh. I sucked all over her calf muscles, then opened her sex lips wide, located her clit, and attacked it like it owed me some money.

Mardi fell on the couch. "Aw, Jahmani. Please, *papi*."

I pushed her knees to her breasts, making her bust her cat wide open, stuck my nose right on her hole, and inhaled as hard as I could before licking in between the folds. "You finna cum on this tongue, Mardi? I know this pussy. I was the first to hit this." I spread her lips wide, exposing her pink, and trailed my tongue in circles around her button, then sucked it into my mouth. Her juices were pouring out of her heavily now.

She arched her back and bit into the arm of the couch. "Aw, Jahmani! Jahmani! You do this shit to me every time!" she screamed and started to shudder, cumming all over my mouth.

I slurped up her secretions, tasted them running down my throat, swallowed, and went back to drink more. My lips were pursed together as if they were extracting juice from a berry. I continued to suck and lick while she came for a second time, licking all over her juicy thighs and all the way down to her ankles.

She closed her eyes tight, then pushed me off her. "Let me suck that dick, *papi*. I need it. Fuck this. You do this to me every time." She climbed from under me and knelt between my legs, pulling my jeans down my thighs and off my ankles. I took my pistol and slid it into the cushions. My boxers were lowered next.

She grabbed my thick penis in her hand and squeezed it. "Damn, *papi*. You done sprouted on me. I don't remember it being this big. She pumped it a few times and licked the head, taking the precum from the helmet and smacking her lips together. "My *papi* taste so good." She sucked my piece into her mouth and trailed her lips up and down it, sucking hard.

Her hot mouth sent tingles through me. The noises were loud and sloppy-sounding. It drove me crazy. I looked down on her pretty ass sucking me like a veteran. I humped into her mouth. My eyes rolled into the back of my head. I shivered and allowed her to do her thing. It felt so good.

My first time ever getting head had been by her. We were only eleven years old. She'd been afraid to let me put it in her kitty back then, even though I had been ready, so all I could do was rub her little box while she bossed me just like this. She said she'd learned from watching her father's pornos and practicing on a lollipop. Thank God for that.

I squeezed my eyelids tight and rose from the couch. She pumped me faster and faster with her left hand, her mouth sucking halfway down my pipe, ready for me to explode.

I dug my nails into the sofa. My toes curled. I felt myself shaking, and then I threw my head back. I couldn't take it anymore. The feeling was too great. I scrunched my face, and then I was cumming. "Fuck, Mardi! I'm cumming, *mami*. I'm cumming!" Spurt after spurt of my seed shot out of me and into her mouth.

She tightened her lips and drank from my fountain. Her throat moved up and down until I was finished, then she popped me out and smiled while running my dick head all over her pretty and soft cheeks.

"I want you to fuck me, *papi*. I need some. My itch ain't been scratched ever since we went on a break. I need you right now."

She stood up and bent over the couch, smacking herself on her right ass cheek, making it jiggle. She slid her right hand under her belly, playing with her glistening brown lips. Cum continued to run out of her and down her thick thighs

I knelt behind her and vacuumed her juices with my lips, sucking on her flesh and tasting her salt. The taste of pussy was so scrumptious to me. I stood behind her and rubbed my dick head up and down her wet slit, then found her hole. I forced her to bend over a little more so that ass was all in my lap the way I needed it to be. Her ass cheeks spread. The crinkle of her asshole winked at me. I bent down to run my tongue in circles around it, then stood back up, guided my dick to the entrance of her pussy, and slammed forward, giving her a nice eight inches. I took ahold of her hips and gave her the last three and a half.

"*Papi*! *Papi*! You gotta take it easy. It's been so long. That's a lot of dick. Please. Let me get used to it again." She said this looking over her shoulder at me.

I smacked that big ass. She yelped. Her juices dripped off my pole and onto the carpet.

"You know how this shit go. I fuck this pussy how I wanna fuck this pussy. I'm *papi*!" I dug my fingers into the flesh of her hips and pulled her back to me hard. I had to close my eyes because they rolled into the back of my head. I got weak at the knees. Her lips seemed to be gripping me like a fist. It felt like we were twelve and screwing for the first time under me and my brother Pacho's bunk bed. "Damn, Mardi, this shit so tight, *mami*. What you been doing to it?" I groaned, stroking her cat at a nice pace, making sure her ass was clapping into my lap.

There was no point in fucking a thick-ass woman if you couldn't feel that booty every single time you hit that thang from the back. Mardi was so thick I had to enjoy that feel. It was another reason she had me so obsessed with her fine ass.

She threw her head all around, and that loosened her ponytail. Her long hair was all over her face. She looked like a wild fucking animal. She took her ass and slammed it into my lap. Her big breasts worked themselves out of her shirt, the nipples heavily engorged. "Fuck me, *papi*! Fuck me! *Papi*! *Papi*! Yes! Hit it! Hit it, *papi*! B-X style! Harder! Harder, *papi*!" She closed her eyes and crashed back into me as hard as she could.

Her pussy felt like a hot, wet, fleshy vacuum cleaner sucking at me. Her ass would crash and jiggle in my lap. I watched my dick slide in and out of her, getting more and more greasy from her innards. My balls crashed into her clit and became drenched with her fluids. I sucked my middle finger and slid it into her asshole, then sped up the pace, working her like the Don was supposed to. I dug deep into her body. "Ugh! Ugh! Ugh! Ugh! Aw, shit, boo! Shit!" I felt my orgasm building.

"*Papi*, I'm finna cum. Take your finger out of my ass. Take it out or I'm finna cum. I'm finna cum all over you! *Papi*!"

I smacked that ass so hard and stabbed into her while digging my middle finger as deep as it could go into her back door. She began to cum, and I did, too. I held her around the waist and pumping until my seed spilled deeply inside her womb, bouncing off her velvety walls. She screamed into the couch pillows and collapsed with her face in the crease of the sofa, leaving my dick throbbing in the air. Her juices leaking off it.

Ghost

I lay on my back while Mardi straddled me and laid her head on my chest. Her right hand traveled up and down my right arm. We were fresh out of the shower and had two slices of pizza apiece in us. I felt her naked breasts mold into my stomach. The heat radiating from her into me felt good. I'd missed just being in close confines with her. Her scent, her touch, her voice. The intimacy of it all had me floating on air, even though a major part of me wanted to rebel against it.

I didn't want to get too comfortable because, throughout our separation, I had become accustomed to being alone, to sleeping with random women where there were no strings or feelings attached. I liked getting what I wanted out of a female and being on my way. I mean, I made it a point to always try to leave them better off than when I'd gotten to 'em, but emotionally I was clogged up and closed off. So many months of thinking the only woman I had ever truly loved had cheated on me and betrayed my trust had caused my heart to become somewhat cold. And now finding out my feelings toward Mardi's betrayal had not, in fact, been her fault was messing with my brain a little bit. It's like I had been mad at her for so long that I was stuck.

She sat upright and the covers slid down her back. Her breasts jiggled on her chest as she looked down at me, her pretty face illuminated by the flickering candles in the room. She licked her juicy lips and smiled. "*Papi*, I'm not used to you being so quiet. What's on your mind? And don't say 'nuthin'', either."

I slid my hands up and placed them on each cheek of her backside. They felt hot and soft in my hands. I could feel a few stretch marks going across them. I squeezed the soft cheeks with my fingers, and relished in their softness. There was nothing like a thick woman in my book. "Nall, ma. I was just thinking to myself that I feel like we fucked up by getting back in the sack so fast. I mean, we ain't even got an understanding about what really went down wit' you back on the island. I mean, I know it's mostly my fault because you was telling me to stop and shit, but I ain't seen you in so long. Then your scent has always driven me crazy. You definitely done got badder. Then it was like, yo, I just had to slap them skins, ma. See what this new body be about. Of course it's a lot of feelings wrapped up inside of me for you, too. So you know how that go." I gripped her cheeks a li'l tighter. The way she had her thighs spread allowed me to feel her kitty on my stomach. It felt so good.

She shook her head. "Dang, *papi*, I thought we was over that." She rolled her eyes and got out of the bed. When she placed her first foot on the floor, her thighs opened, and the light from the candle allowed me to catch another glimpse of her bald kitty before she stepped into her white boy short panties and pulled them up. Her breasts jiggled throughout the whole process.

My piece was throbbing hard. I was trying to not focus in on what I was seeing or the yearning in my loins, but it was a difficult task because, as much as I hated to admit it, I had a thing for Mardi, and probably always would.

She slid her tank top over her breasts, then paced back and forth in the dark room. Sometimes she would step into the candle's light, and other times she was in pure darkness. Her shadow cast over the walls.

"I mean, I don't know what to say, Jahmani. I fucked up. The woman in me won't allow for myself to put it all on my cousin and her man because I kind of knew what they were hinting at before I started drinking with them. I knew better. That didn't give her the right to put something in my tequila, though. I still don't even know what it was. All I know is I was screwed up after that. I was slurring my words and feeling more sexual than I ever remember feeling before. Before I could comprehend what was going on inside of my head, her boyfriend was kissing me, and she was cheering him on. She literally helped him take most of my clothes off. I mean, I put up a fight, but I couldn't honestly tell you how much of a fight I really put up because most of that night is kind of lost in the back of my brain somewhere. I can recall both of them being naked. Doing things to me. There was a lot of kissing and touching. Then he was on top of me, doing his thing. I passed out during the process. When I woke up, it was the next afternoon. I had a pounding headache, and my downstairs ached. Both he and my cousin were in the bed, one on each side of me, and they were both naked. I got up and snapped out, fought with them for a full hour, then went right to the doctor and got tested. I found out I was clean, and then I filed a police report against him. They came and got him later that day, and I haven't spoken to my cousin or any family back home ever since then." She sighed and continued to pace. "I mean, that's everything. So, what more do you want from me? I feel bad enough." She stopped and knelt by the bed, looking up at me.

I was playing with the curls on top of my head. Every time I imagined another nigga between her thighs, it got me madder and madder. For so long I had been the only one who got that opportunity. Now that another man had, I was feeling angry and a little sick on the stomach. Mardi had been my heart.

I lowered my head and shook it just a bit. "Yo, ma, my word, I didn't know it went down like that. My moms ain't say nothing about you calling the law and all that shit. If you took it that far, then that had to be rough for you. That's my bad, because I really didn't understand. I just been vexed for so long that it's kinda spilling over even though you're telling me what's really good." I pulled her up and wrapped my arms around her. "I'm sorry you had to go through that. And I'm sorry for not being man enough to really find out what took place. You know I got mad love for you, goddess. Have since day one. Gimme some."

She wrapped her arms around my neck and turned her head slightly to the side before kissing my lips. Hers felt like soft, warm pillows that had been fluffed just for me. Her spit tasted like mouthwash. I rubbed all over her booty, giving her a wedgie by the time I was done with it.

"*Papi*, I love you. I know we got some repairing to do, but do you think there is any chance of us being able to get back together? Be honest with me?"

"Yo, I don't see why not. Long as you keeping it one hunnit wit' me, you already know how my love for you is. I been missing you ever since we parted. But just on some real shit, you know I ain't stop getting ass, so I got some ties to sever."

She wiggled out of my embrace and crossed her arms. "Dang, who you been laying down wit'? I hope you used protection, 'cause we definitely didn't." She frowned and her eyes got low.

I stood up and pulled her back to me. "Chill yo' ass out. I got this. I made sure I strapped up and hit my doctor every three months faithfully. I respect myself too much not to." I kissed her forehead. "But just for all intents and purposes, let's just hold fast on the whole relationship end of things until we can get our lives back aligned with each others. I'm sure you got a few niggas you jamming wit', too."

"No! I ain't fucked with nobody outside of you other than that one bad experience. I ain't never been a ho. You know that." She stormed out of the bedroom. "Maybe you should just get dressed and leave. I can't deal with this right now. Hit me up when you're ready to be serious. I'm on some elevation-type shit. I ain't got time for nothing else."

Chapter 5

I took one of the paper fans that the church handed out to the congregation as we came through the doors and fanned my face with it. I was hot as hell and sweating. Me and my mother had been at the service for two and a half hours, and thankfully it was coming to a close. I didn't understand how a Catholic service had somehow been intermingled with that of a Baptist one. Her church services never lasted more than an hour. But this Sunday their church had a pastor visiting, along with his choir, from New Jersey, and I was somehow caught in the middle of it. I was hot, irritated, and ready to go. It wasn't that I didn't believe in God, because I most certainly did. I just wasn't the type to do the whole church thing. I felt me and God had a strong understanding right here in my heart. So yeah, I was ready to go a long time ago.

Finally, after four hours, the out-of-town pastor had us stand, and he said the final prayer and dismissed us. I felt like I'd been freed from prison. I wiped the sweat from my brow one final time and dropped the fan on the pew on my way out of the door when my mother grabbed my forearm.

"Boy, can you just hold up for a second? Let me make my rounds and we can get out of here." She rubbed my face and headed to the front of the church where the dark-skinned, slim, bald out-of-town pastor was hugging some of the other church members.

I was so irritated I wanted to kick something. I picked my paper fan back up and wagged it over my face, searching for temporary relief and receiving barely any.

"Excuse me, can I get past you?" came the soft voice of a female.

Before I could turn around, I smelled her intoxicating perfume. I turned around and looked into the face of a caramel-skinned female of about nineteen or twenty years old.

She had brown eyes and shoulder-length hair that was wavy. She looked as if she weighed about 140 pounds, no taller than 5'5", and she was giving me just enough smile to showcase her deep dimples. There were freckles on her beautiful face as well, which was odd to me because I had never seen a black female with freckles unless they were very light skinned, which she was not. I couldn't stop looking at her. She was that fine to me.

She frowned. "Uh, are you alright? Did you hear what I said? I'm trying to get past you."

I snapped out of it. "Aw, man, that's my bad. Yeah, go ahead." I turned to the side so she could squeeze by me.

She brushed past me just close enough so I could feel her warm arm. She wore a blue and yellow dress over yellow red-bottomed heels. She took one more look up at me before she took a few more paces down the row we were standing in, knelt, and crossed her chest with the sign of the crucifix before closing her eyes and placing her hands together in prayer. I could see her lips moving, and I swear I could not stop looking at this girl. I don't know what was wrong with me. I was stuck. I mean, there was nothing out of the ordinary about her, yet I was lost in time.

My mother came behind me and placed her hand on my shoulder. "Okay, baby, I've talked to everybody I need to. We can get out of here before you lose your mind." She stood on her tippy-toes and kissed my cheek.

I heard what she was saying, but I couldn't take my eyes off the female who had passed me. "Mama, you know almost everybody in this church, right?" I asked, not taking my eyes off the female. I could feel the sweat dripping off me, and I didn't care. I had to know who she was. I wasn't leaving that church until I found out.

"Yeah. Well, mostly everybody. I don't know the ones

from this Baptist church, though they do throw a good service. Why baby?"

I nodded my head toward the praying woman. "Her right there, who is she? I need to know. She got me feeling some type of way. I'm serious."

My mother stood beside me and bucked her eyes. "Aw, nall baby, don't you worry about who she is. That information is not good for you." She grabbed my hand and started to pull me away.

"What?" I took my hand out of her grasp and stood firm. "Who is she? I wanna know now."

The female took some rosary beads out of her purse and began to pray with them. Her lips began to move again, but now there were tears streaming down her pretty face.

My mother took my hand and interlocked our fingers. "Do you remember the man that was killed inside of my building? You know, the one they found inside the boiler room, in the incinerator?" She looked up to me and gave me a weary smile.

"Yeah, I remember hearing about that." I said this while still watching the woman closely. I wanted to go over and put my arms around her. I didn't know why she was crying, but I wanted to heal her as best I could. Something in me yearned to do it.

"Well, my son, that is his sister. Her name is Ari, and she goes to this church. Please stay away from her, son. I am begging you." She tried to pull me away again.

My heart dropped into my stomach. Mikey did have a sister, but she couldn't have been her. How could any woman who looked like she did have a brother who looked like he did? Then my mother's last words hit me. "Wait, why are you begging me to stay away from her? What's your deal with this woman?" I asked, still not taking my eyes away from Ari. She kissed her rosary and continued to pray as if she was the only one left in the building.

My mother pulled on my wrist. "Just forget about it baby. Let's go. Please." She looked over to Ari.

Ari stood up and wiped her cheeks. She dabbed at her eyes with a tissue and proceeded to make her way down the row. There was just a major pulling on me. I needed to say something to her, needed to ask her how she was doing or something. I had never felt that way about anybody. The urge to meet her was so strong I felt like if I didn't, I would be sick.

I broke away from my mother and made my way down the aisle, catching her right before she headed out the door of the church. "Ari! Ari! Hold up," I hollered, jogging over to her.

She froze in place and looked over her shoulder at me, confused. "Uh, do I know you?" she asked. Even though her face was turned into a slight frown, her dimples were popping. Sweat glistened on her forehead. I could see traces of it peppered on her chest through the opening in her dress.

I shook my head. "Nall, you don't know me, but I just had to say something to you. First, are you okay? I saw you crying back there." I pointed over my shoulder with my thumb.

She jerked her head back. "I'm fine. I was talking to our Father in Heaven. Sometimes it makes me emotional. Is that a crime?"

I shook my head. "Nall, of course not. I just. I don't know. But, like I said, I just had to say something to you. You are beautiful, and I have never in my life seen anybody as gorgeous as you are. I mean, I saw you down there praying, and I wanted to say something to you then, but that would have been –"

She held up her hand to stop me. "Dude, this ain't cool. I don't know you. I don't like you. And I think you're bogus for trying to come at me in God's house. I think it'll be in your best interest to step away. Have some decency about yourself.

I'm not interested." She rolled her eyes, grabbed the handle to the church's door again, and stepping out of it.

I stood there perplexed for a full minute before I followed her outside. I was thinking I needed to apologize to her. Maybe I was bogus for coming at her in the Lord's house. That had to seem pretty thirsty. Then I had asked her why she'd been crying. Damn, I messed up that whole thing. I had to make it right.

I threw open the church's double doors and stepped out into the hot August humidity. It felt like it was a million degrees outside. I looked to my right and saw a bunch of the churchgoers headed to their cars or already in there cars, driving away. There were two groups of them headed toward the church's big parking lot. I scanned the entire area and could not locate Ari, so I looked to my left. Down that street, by the grace of God, I saw her. She was hugging some older woman with a big hat, then knelt and hugged the little girl who had been holding the older woman's hand before getting up and walking across the street. She pulled out here cell phone and placed it to her ear.

My mother came from behind me. "Are you ready to go now. I need to put something on my stomach."

"Hold on, Mama. I just gotta do this one thing." I took off running in the direction of Ari. I watched her turn the corner and keep on walking. I was trying to rehearse in my head what I was going to say to her this time. I knew I was going to start with an apology, for sure. Hopefully that would be an ice breaker. After she accepted my apology, I would start over, and maybe invite her to dinner or something.

The reality that I had been the one to kill her brother never even crossed my mind as I was running over to her. All I could see was me talking to her again. It was like I needed to so bad.

I waited until two cars drove past before I was able to cross the same street she had. I could hear my mother calling my name behind me, but I ignored her. I couldn't allow her to hold me back. I had to do this. I had to try again with this woman. Her spirit was calling out to me. At least that was how I was feeling.

By the time I got to the corner, she had completely disappeared around it, but I closed the ground between us real fast. When I got to the corner, I saw her stop by the driver's side of a midnight-blue Lexus truck. She chirped the alarm and popped the door from her keys.

"Ari! Wait a minute." I jogged over to the back of her truck and stopped to catch my breath. My heart was beating fast in my chest. Sweat poured down my back, and I could feel my shirt sticking to me.

"Man, what is your problem, homie? I thought I told you back there that wasn't nothin' happening. Why are you following me? Are you some kind of crazed lunatic or somethin'?" She opened her driver's door all the way.

I came around her truck, still breathing hard. I knew I had to look crazy as hell, all out of breath and sweaty like that. it was not my best moment, but I just had to let her know what I was feeling. "Okay." I held up a hand, trying to catch my breath. "First, I just wanted to apologize for how I came at you back there. You're right. We were at church, and I shouldn't have been trying to pick you up. Secondly, I still think you are the most beautiful woman I have ever seen in my life. If you'll give me a chance, I would like to take you out to dinner so I can get to know you."

She scrunched her face. "What part of what I said back there don't you get up here?" She tapped the side of her head, "Huh? I said I wasn't feeling you. I'm not on that. I got too much going on in my life right now. And besides that, you ain't my type. I'm not interested. Have a good day." She sat in her truck and got ready to close the door.

"Yo, I'm sorry about your brother!" I don't know how that came out of my mouth. I panicked. Damn, I panicked.

Her driver's door was on its way to closing, but when she heard that she opened it and stepped back out. "What did you say about my brother?" She was in the street now, walking toward me. For the first time I noticed she had gloves on that went all the way up to her biceps. They matched her dress and made her swag really go through the roof.

I looked into her eyes. "I said I'm sorry about your brother. My mother told me what happened, and I just wanted to convey my condolences."

She walked in a little closer and looked up at me. "I don't need your condolences or your sympathy. My brother was a street nigga. He lived by the gun. The Bible says if you live by the sword, you'll die by it. So, it is what it is. I'm dealing with it. I wish I knew who did it, though. Can't wait until I find out who did. Unless that's the reason you're pursuing me so heavily, because you know? Well, do you?"

Now I was stuttering my words like damn fool. "Naw, I was just. I mean, if I did, I would probably. But."

As I was trying to get my words together, three blue Navigators pulled into the middle of the street and stopped a short distance away from us. Their doors opened up, and what looked like more than fifteen dudes got out with blue bandanas around their necks and tattoos all over their faces and arms. One of them in particular, a big muscle-bound, light-skinned dude with long dreads, walked toward us. Before I could move, he pulled two chrome .45s out of his waistband and aimed them at me. I could see they were already cocked and ready to go. He had a mean mug on his face, along with plenty of tattoos.

I was stuck. I'd left my .9 millimeter in the truck before

I'd gone into the church. I held my hands shoulder-high and cursed under my breath. I was expecting to be robbed. "Yo, I got, like, a gee on me, homie. You can have that shit, just let me keep my life. That's all I ask."

Before he could make it to me, four of his goons rushed me and slammed me on the hood of a Buick Century that was parked behind Ari's truck. The impact knocked the wind out of me. Then the big monster grabbed me by the neck and put his gun to my forehead.

"Who the fuck are you, and where do you get off talking to my muthafucking li'l cousin?" he growled.

Ari rushed over to his side. "Mach, this is crazy. There are people all around. He was just making sure I made it safe to my car. That's it. That's all. I swear," she pleaded.

Mach curled his top lip. "Answer me, bitch-nigga, or I'ma splash yo' ass right here, Baltimore-style. Word is bond."

I felt him press the barrel under my chin. That shit had me so heated I was seeing stars. My blood pressure was through the roof, I could tell. "Yo, get yo' fucking gun from under my chin, kid. You heard what she said. These streets crazy. I just wanted to make sure she made it to her whip safe. What's the harm in that?" I asked, lying because I was trapped in an impossible situation. I didn't know who this nigga was or where he came from, but the only thing that kept going through my mind was that I was going to catch and murder him one day. I wasn't feeling this shit at all. I was wishing I'd never pursued Ari now. I mean, she was bad, but it wasn't worth this.

He grabbed a handful of my shirt. "Oh, so you one of them tough, mixed niggas, huh? Bitch-nigga, where set you claim, cuz?"

"What?" I asked. I knew this big dummy wasn't gang-banging at a time like this. That messed me up. "Excuse me?"

"Mach, let him up. What are you doing? Are you trying to go back to prison? You just got out," Ari shouted, pulling his arm backward. "You acting like an idiot. There are people with their phones out recording this. Damn!"

"Nigga, red or blue? Tell me right the fuck now," he frowned and pressed his barrel into my skin again.

I looked him in the eyes and curled my lip. "Nigga, fuck you! Stop playing around with that gun and pull the trigger," I spat.

"Aw, cuz, I see Twelve! Fuck that bitch-nigga. We'll see him around," one of the members of his crew hollered before jogging back to his truck.

Mach raised his head to look down the street. As soon as he did, I swung with all of my might and connected with his jaw. My knuckles crashed into the bone and dropped him. He fell into the middle of the street, and I took off running right past the churchgoers who were on their way to their whips. My fist was throbbing.

***

My ma set a bowl of ice on the table, shaking her head. "I told you to not say nothing to that girl. I told you she was trouble. But you never listen, son. Damn! Why are you so freaking hard-headed?" she asked, smacking me in the back of the head.

I buried my right fist in the bowl of ice and winced in pain. It had swollen up from the connection. I could barely close it, but I didn't care. That punk had that coming. I wasn't about to let no nigga snatch me up like that. I was a man before anything else, first and foremost. "Ma, it was just one of those things. I had to say something to her. I couldn't help it."

"What type of boy wants to talk to the girl of the man he

murdered? That doesn't make sense to me. You're crazy!" She picked up a joint and popped it into her mouth, lighting the end of it and inhaling deeply.

I faced her and tilted my head to the side. "Who told you that?"

"Told me what, Jahmani? What are you talking about?" She avoided eye contact with me. "Just soak your fist, baby, and be cool."

I slammed my hand on the table. "Stop playing with me, Mama. Who told you I killed anybody?" I felt my temper rising.

She looked up at me and scooted her chair back. She held the joint in the corner of her mouth with smoke rising from it. "You think I'm scared of your loud bangs and angry face? Huh? Do you? Well, let me tell you something, Jahmani. I held you in my stomach for nine months and pushed you out of my womb. If it was not for me, you'd not be here. I brought you here, and I'll kill you if I ever grow scared of you. You got me? Now, I said be cool. Change the subject, or I'll fuck you up. I'm from San Juan. I sliced all of my brothers, you remember?" She pointed at me and took her seat, crossing her thighs.

My mother had told me the stories about how her brothers had a habit of putting their hands on her when they were growing up. She had three of them, and they didn't stop putting their hands on her until she'd stabbed each and every one of them, leaving scars that were eight inches long, three at a time. One of my uncles had two slices across his face that my mother had given him. I knew about the ordeals, but in that moment I didn't care.

"Do you believe I killed Ari's brother? Huh, Mama?" There was more than one way to skin a deer. I knew that once my mother started talking, she would expose her source. I just had to pay attention and listen attentively.

She shrugged her shoulders. "I don't care if you did. It's a part of the game. I'd rather it be him than you any day. Besides, he was a bad man, robbing even old women from this building. He got what he deserved. Nobody is going to lose any sleep over his death, other than Ari. He had no right putting his hands on my granddaughter. You should have killed him. *To the dust with such filth*," she shouted in Spanish.

Bingo! It couldn't be anybody other than Samantha who could have told her what happened. I nodded my head. Samantha never could keep her mouth closed. She seemed to tell my mother everything sooner or later. I took my seat. "Mama, forgive me for raising my voice to you. I love you, and you are my queen. Never forget that."

She laughed. "Boy, you better watch that bipolar shit. One minute you're the sweetest piece of son-candy in the world, then the next you're bitter as a rotten apple. I don't know whether to love you or kick your ass. Give me kisses, baby. You know I am only playing with you."

I came over and kissed both of her cheeks, then her forehead. "I love you, my angel. I got a lot of studying to do, and then I gotta hit up the slums to see if I can come up on some chump change. Hit my phone if you need anything. Okay?"

She nodded and smiled. "Okay, baby. Hit those lights on your way out. And Jahmani? Please, stay away from that girl. She is trouble. Her whole family seems to be under the umbrella of Satan." She waved me off. "Later."

Ghost

Chapter 6

Samantha answered the door five minutes later with a bottle of Cîroc in her hand. The first thing I noticed was her nails were done, and so was her makeup. She was dressed in a tight-fitting Coogi dress that showed off all of her thighs. Her hair flowed down her back.

She smiled, rushed me, and wrapped her arms around me. "Bro, damn, I been missing yo' ass. Come on in. I'm in here cooking." She stepped back into the house. "Close that door behind you."

My eyes had a mind of their own. As she walked away, I looked down and saw the way her ass was jiggling under the Coogi dress. Every step she took caused it to raise a bit higher. I shook my head and closed the door. I could feel a cool breeze coming from the house, and that made me smile. On top of that, it was clean. I couldn't see any roaches or rats just yet. I took that as a good sign.

It smelled like tacos. My stomach growled. "Damn, what smell so good in here?" I asked, looking toward the back of the house where Lonnie's room was.

Samantha was dancing in front of the stove, stirring the ground beef that was sizzling in a skillet. She sprinkled a pinch of taco seasoning on top of it and smiled. "Well, I was in a good mood, so I figured I'd whip me and my daughter up some tacos and whatnot. I haven't cooked in a while." She dropped some more seasoning into the skillet. "Why, are you hungry?"

My stomach was growling like crazy, but I still couldn't get the sight of how her crib usually was out of my mind. I mean, I was accustomed to living in the projects because I had my whole life, but still, I never got used to it. "Nall, I'm good. But thank you for asking."

She raised her eyebrow. "What? Boy, yeah right. Huh,

taste this." She scooped some of the meat up with a wooden spoon and brought it over to me. "You ain't never tasted my cooking. Trust me, I do my thing. You know how we get down in Brooklyn."

"Yeah, whatever." I ate the meat off the spoon and chewed it up, switching it from one side of my mouth to the other because it was so hot. I had to admit the flavor was amazing. My taste buds felt like they were trying to explode. I had to bend over and hold my jaws. Damn it was good. "Yo, you a monster, Ma! Word is bond."

She was back at the stove, cooking, popped back on her legs. "Yeah, I already know. So, what brings you here? You missed me?"

I scoffed and laughed at her ass. "Before I get on that, where is my princess? I miss her."

She rolled her eyes and pointed. "She in my room, asleep. You can go back there and see. It's good. Before you come back, make sure you try to muster some of that puttiness for me. Shid, I told you I missed you. The least you could do is miss me a little bit. Damn."

I crept through the small apartment and made my way to Samantha's bedroom, twisted the knob, and pushed the door inward. Her television was on with the volume turned down. I looked to her dresser and saw what looked like a pound of weed. Next to it was a small handgun and a plate with cocaine on top of it.

Lonnie lay in the middle of the bed with a sheet pulled over her, snoring lightly. I climbed onto it and lowered myself in a push-up position, rubbed my cheek against hers, and then kissed it. It felt soft and warm. She smelled of baby lotion.

"Princess? Princess? Wake up, baby. I wanna see your pretty face," I cooed into her little ear.

Her eyes moved behind her eyelids, and then she opened

them. Her eyes were crossed at first until they focused themselves. "Uncle? Uncle, is that you?" She turned and looked up at me.

I kissed her lips and pulled her up, wrapping her into my arms. "Yeah it's me, baby. How are you doing?"

She struggled to wake up. Her arms hugging my neck tightly. "I missed you." Her voice was raspy. Her breath smelled a little funny. Not bad, but not fresh either. But it didn't bother me at all. She was my heart.

"I missed you, too. You gon' come and spend the weekend with me this week, okay?" I held her tighter.

She nodded her head with her face against mine. We were cheek-to-cheek. "I would love that. I can't wait." Her eyes closed.

I lowered her back to the bed and laid her head on the pillow, kissing her cheek. Then it hit me that there were drugs and a gun in the room. I picked her up and carried her into her bedroom, kicked the door open, and laid her in her bed. I took a five dollar bill out of my pocket and put it into her little hand, closing her fist around it. "I love you, princess, and I'll see you later this week, if not earlier."

I kissed her again and stepped out of her bedroom. Samantha was just coming out of the kitchen with the bottle of Cîroc in her right hand.

"Is she still asleep, Jahmani? I know she should be. She was up all night. I think –"

I grabbed her by the throat and slammed her into the wall. The bottle of Cîroc dropped to the floor and rolled across the carpet, spilling liquor all over it. Her eyes were opened big. She started to shake.

"Shorty, are you out of yo' rabid-ass mind? Huh? What the fuck is wrong wit' you?" I snapped, feeling my body get hot. My heart was beating fast in my chest.

"What are you talking about, Jahmani? What did I do?" she asked, shaking. She gagged and smacked at the hand around her throat because I had tightened it again.

I smacked her swatting hand away and picked her up off her feet with one arm, heated. I was choking her and wasn't sure if I was going to kill her right there or not. I squeezed for a full thirty seconds, watched her face turn red before I dropped her to the carpet and picked her up, grabbing a handful of her hair. "You got my muthafucking niece sleeping in a room where there is cocaine on a plate, weed in saran, and a pistol. A muthafucking pistol?" I smacked her across the face, and dropped her to the carpet again. "You think this shit a game?"

She fell onto her bottom and tried to get up to flee the room. "I'm sorry! I'm sorry! I wasn't thinking! She was asleep!" she hollered.

I grabbed a handful of her hair and flung her back to me, then pushed her to the couch. I took my Gucci belt out of its loop holes and held the buckle in my right hand. I took a seat on the cushions and pulled her over my lap, pulling her Coogi dress all the way up, exposing the blue thong that separated her butt cheeks. Since she wanted to act like a child and do childish shit, I was gon' treat her like one.

She kicked her legs wildly and tried to fight her way out of my grasp. "Wait! Please, Jahmani, don't do this. I wasn't thinking. I'll go move all of that stuff right now. I just got it," she hollered and continued to kick her legs.

With all of the moving, I wound up dropping the belt so I could catch her legs. I placed them between my thighs, and trapped her so she couldn't move from the waist down. I pulled that Coogi dress up so far it was on her lower back. "I'm tired of having to tell you how to behave as a woman. You got a five-year-old daughter that's watching everything you do. You are her role model. I'll be damned if you keep this bullshit up." I smacked her on the ass with my bare hand as hard as I could, right on the left cheek. It shook. I raised my hand again and smacked the right one just as hard.

She cocked her head back and howled. "Aw! Jahmani! Please, bro. I swear to God, I won't mess up no more. I wasn't thinking."

Smack! Smack! Smack! "That's yo' problem, you ain't never thinking. You got a whole-ass daughter! That's the first thing you need to do before you make a decision!" *Smack! Smack!* My hand slammed into those cheeks with no mercy. Before I could calm down, my hand was going crazy on that ass. Again and again, relentlessly.

She wiggled this way and that. Somehow she'd managed to come from between my legs, but I trapped her again and held her down. Her ass cheeks were a crimson color, the dress all the way around her waist. "Please! Please. Aw, it hurts so bad. I'm begging you, Jahmani. I'm begging you." She broke into a fit of tears, sobbing against my thighs, rubbing her face all over them. "I'm so, so sorry."

I wasn't letting up that easily. I felt like she needed her ass whooped, and instead of me beating her like most trifling-ass niggas would have done, I decided to get in her ass this way. Make it hard for her to sit down for a few days. I was tearing them cheeks up. *Smack! Smack! Smack!* Hitting her harder and harder. My hand was steaming from her skin.

She bit into the denim of my jeans and continued to sob while I beat that tail for three minutes straight. It went from her jumping around like crazy and screaming to her just lying there and rubbing her face all over my pants leg. She stopped groaning and started to moan deep within her throat, opening her thighs and grinding into my leg.

This kind of shocked me. I thought it was a ploy to get me

to stop, so I kept on spanking that ass until I was done. Then I pushed her off my lap. She fell to the carpet on her side, tears streaming down her face. Her right hand went between her legs and into her panties. I could tell because her dress was around her stomach. She closed her eyes and slid two fingers into her box, working them in and out of her hole, moaning out loud.

"Why'd you do that? Why did you have to do that, Jahmani?" She fell to her back and opened her thighs wide. Her fingers plunged in and out of her faster and faster. She pulled the panties all the way to one side so she could really go at herself. "Uh! Damn you. Damn you, Jahmani. You ain't right. I swear you ain't right."

I felt so guilty because I was hard as hell. I mean, my piece was jumping in my jeans, but this was my brother's baby mother, so I had to snap out of that lustful zone. I jumped up and fixed my dick so it was laid up against my stomach, the big helmet peeking out of my waistband. She opened her eyes as I was doing so and caught me.

"Yo, Samantha, chill out, ma!. Take yo' ass in the room and do that. You know that ain't right."

She pulled her fingers out of herself and emitted a sucking sound from her box. That sent a chill down my spine. I looked between her legs and saw how swollen her kitty was. It had a clear gel running out of it, wetting her ass cheeks.

"Don't leave me like this, Jahmani. Please, don't leave me like this. At least touch this. I swear I won't say shit. Just touch me right here." She smushed her pussy lips together and squeezed out more of the gel, then ran her fingers up and down her slit, sliding a middle finger into herself.

My dick was going crazy. I was shaking, I was so horny just watching her thick-ass. "Yo, I can't do Pacho like that. That's my brother. I love that fool. And I respect you more

66

than that."

She shook her head. "It ain't about no fucking respect right now, Jahmani. I'm hurting. I need some. You got me riled up. You know I got daddy issues, then you gon' spank me. What did you expect me to behave like?" She got on her knees and crawled across the floor, running her hand up and down my pants front. I could smell the pussy on her, mixed with her perfume. Her hand felt heavy and warm. Her thumb grazed the head of my piece.

I closed my eyes and clenched my teeth. "Yo, fo' real, Samantha. Back yo' ass up, girl." Those were the words that came out of my mouth, but I didn't make any attempt to push her away. I was horny and in need of some pussy. Everything in me was screaming for me to get out of there, though.

She opened my pants and grabbed my log. "Damn, Jahmani, stop playing. Look how hard you are. You want some of me just like I want some of you." She stroked my pipe. "Just let me put it in my mouth one time. I swear, you'll be hooked. This Brooklyn's finest, right here." She kissed the head that was sticking out of my waistband, then licked it. "Uh! Please fuck me." Her left hand was between her legs, fingering her wet box. I could hear it slipping around inside of her. It was tempting.

I don't know where I got the strength from, but I pushed her away and took a step back. "Nall, shorty, I ain't going to. I can't do bro like this. I got more love for kid than this."

She fell on her back and opened her legs, fingering herself faster and faster. "Okay, just let me look at it, then. I ain't had no dick since Mikey, and he came so fast I couldn't do nothing. Just let me look, Jahmani. Looking can't hurt. Take it out. Please." She ran her hand over the stretch marks on her stomach and continued to handle her business.

My pants were open, my piece sticking out of it like a log.

The more I watched her, the more it jumped. Man, if Pacho wasn't my brother, I would have been knee-deep in her bad ass. I knelt down and brought it closer to her. She wrapped her hand around it, squeezing it, then stroking it before she laid it on her cheek and came all over her fingers, smearing her juices over my helmet. I almost came from the taboo aspect of it.

Twenty minutes later I was holding my niece and helping her fold a burrito while Samantha eyed me from across the table as if she was hungry for my flesh or something. "Yo, why you keep looking at me ma? You a'ight?" I asked, placing the burrito in Lonnie's hand. "Here you go, princess."

Lonnie took the burrito and bit into it. Salsa and sour cream stained her cheeks. She smacked loudly. I kissed her on the temple and felt so in love with her. She was my world.

"Nah, I was just tripping by how similar you two look. It's like me and you laid down and made her or something. I mean she favor Pacho a li'l bit, but for the most part she's your twin. That's spooky." She shook her head and bit into her own burrito.

"You should be trying to wonder how you gon' explain to me why you told my moms about Mikey. I thought you was smarter than that." I scoffed and wiped Lonnie's face. I felt good holding her in my arms. I wished she really was my daughter, but then again maybe not. I would have wanted to be in a better position and have more to offer her as a provider. I felt like she deserved the world, and if it was up to me, I would have given it to her with no hesitation. Even though she wasn't my daughter, she was my niece, and I was gon' make it happen for her one day soon. I just felt it.

Samantha dropped her burrito and covered her mouth with her hand. "Oh my God, she told you that I told her about that?"

I wanted to jump across the table and get into her ass, but

luckily I was holding Lonnie. "Nall, she didn't. You just did."

Samantha scooted away from the table and stood up. "I don't know what I was thinking. I just needed to tell somebody, and she's the only one I trust. I didn't think she would say anything, though. I told her that in confidence."

I held the cup full of apple juice to Lonnie's lips. "Who else did you tell?" I glared at her.

"Pacho, but that's it. I swear." She set her plate on the stove.

Now I was heated. I kissed Lonnie on the cheek. "Baby, take this plate in your room so I can finish talking to Mommy. I'll be in there in a minute, okay?"

She nodded and stood up. "Okay, Uncle. Please don't leave without saying bye. I'ma miss you." She hugged my legs and picked up her burrito, spilling most of it on the floor and not noticing.

I grabbed a broom and dust pan, cleaning up the mess. "Yo, I'm seconds away from smacking the fuck outta you, shorty. What would make you tell Pacho anything about that day? Huh?"

She backed into a corner and shrugged her shoulders. "That's my baby daddy. He asked me what happened in our building and why I was all fucked up. Then Lonnie blurted out that a man had beat us up and you beat him up. What was I supposed to do?"

I stood up and dumped the trash from mopping up Lonnie's mess. I grabbed her by the shoulders and held her. "Ma, you doing a whole lot of running your mouth like this shit won't get us put up under the jail for the rest of our natural lives. Shut the fuck up, and don't tell nobody else. Do you hear me? Shut up." I shook her ass and pushed her backward.

She closed her eyes and sucked on her bottom lip. "Okay. I won't no more. Damn." She hugged herself and rubbed her arms, then stepped back to me. "Jahmani, why you be handling me like you do? You got me feeling some type of way. I can't control myself when I'm around you. Can't we just lay down one time so it can get out of my system? I'ma keep making mistakes until I'm able to think straight."

She tried to wrap her arms around me. I placed the palm of my hand on her forehead. "Nah, shorty, no dice. You gotta be more of a woman than you are to get a run at the god. You ain't nothing but a fine-ass li'l girl. I need more than that. Where you get that gun and dope from?"

She turned her back on me and walked into the living room. "I don't want to get into all of that. You ain't gon' do nothing but whoop my ass. I ain't got time for that shit. Damn."

I followed her into the living room and grabbed her by the hair. "Shorty, I ain't playing wit 'you. What's good?"

"Stop, dang, Jahmani. I'm not your woman. I'm Pacho's. I ain't gotta answer to you," she cried.

I tossed her ass to the couch. "Ma, on my word, if you make me ask you again, I'ma fuck you up. Now, I don't want to do that with my niece in here, but you're forcing my hand." I pulled on her hair some more.

"Okay! I'm just serving a li'l bag for the Dyse Avenue Crips. I pop a few pounds for them a week, and they pay my rent each month, and utilities. I ain't gotta fuck nobody, and I don't start officially until Monday. Please don't snap on me."

I grabbed her up by her hair and placed my nose against hers. "Bitch, now you selling dope out of where Lonnie lay her head? Really? I thought I gave you enough to pay up your rent for the year?"

"You did, but I lost it. Somebody kicked in my door while you were in the hospital and took it. What was I supposed to do?"

Her tears only made me ten times more heated. I wanted to fuck her up, but she made this face, and she looked just like Lonnie. As soon as I saw Lonnie's image in her, all of the fight in me left. I slowly let her hair go. "Shorty, you know what? I ain't about to go there with you. You're right, you're not my baby mother. You're Pacho's. So do you. I don't give a fuck. But my niece ain't staying here until you get your shit together. I'ma take her to my mother's. Once I get my chips all the way right, I'ma take her on myself." I stood up and backed away from her. "And I guess that li'l cocaine on the plate, you tooting that shit now, huh?"

She pulled her knees up to her chest and wrapped her arms around them while she sat with her back against the couch. Her silence was enough of an answer for me. I went into Lonnie's room and got her dressed. As soon as she was ready, I picked her up and held her on my hip.

Samantha was still sitting on the floor in the corner of the living room with a few roaches crawling all around her. Tears streamed down her face and dropped off her chin. "I'm sorry, Lonnie. Baby, I'm so sorry. Mama really tried. I really tried, baby." She rocked back and forth, sobbing loudly. Snot ran out of her nose. "Please forgive me."

I shook my head at her and opened the door to her apartment. "Shorty, all them tears get old. You can only be forgiven so many times before shit just get sad. That's what you are right now, real sad. Lonnie, tell your mother you love her."

"I love you, Mama. I'll be back. You don't have to cry, okay?"

Samantha rocked back and forth faster, then she jumped up and ran into the back of the apartment, slamming her bedroom door. "I'm tryin'! Lord knows I'm tryin'! Now he gon' take my baby!" she screamed.

I stood there in the doorway for a few moments, bouncing Lonnie up and down on my hip slightly. A part of me wanted to go in there and console Samantha, but the anger in me wouldn't allow it.

"Uncle, is my mama gon' be okay?" Lonnie asked, tightening her hold around my neck and placing her cheek against mine. I closed the door and nodded. "Yeah, princess. She just need a time-out. Sometimes even parents need a time-out."

Chapter 7

Now that Lonnie was under my care, it meant I was going to have to provide for her as best I could. I never knew how demanding parenting and providing for a little girl was until I took the reigns. Since I'd left her mother's apartment in a bit of anger, I'd managed to neglect grabbing any clothes or any of the necessities she needed, which meant I had to get everything from scratch, including her clothes. I had a thousand dollars to my name after paying all of my mother's bills for the month, so that meant I had to get a move on before I could get Lonnie right, which I fully intended on doing.

Two days after I'd taken Lonnie away from Samantha, I was in my mother's living room studying for my upcoming law enforcement written test for school. I was seated on the floor on my laptop, Lonnie laying against me, playing away on her tablet that I'd purchased for $150 earlier that day.

My mother was in the bathroom showering when there was a knock on her front door. I got up and looked through the peephole with my hand on the handle of my Glock .9. Living in the Bronx River Houses, a nigga always had to be on point. I could never be too careful when it came to answering the door, and I never was. I placed my eye on the peephole, geeked and worried at the same time when I saw my cousin Linx standing in front of the door with his long dreads covering his face. He moved them out of the way and smiled.

"Yo, son, I know you in there. I just got off the phone wit' my aunt, so open the door and give me some love. Word up." He smiled, showing off his mouth full of gold with rubies on each tooth.

My cousin Linx was a pure animal, born and bred in the slums of Brooklyn. He was a project kid just like myself, but instead of graduating high school and taking the college route, he was known for robbing kingpins and moving kilos of heroin. He was a Blood nigga, crazy about everything red. He had been my best friend when we were kids. I'd spent my summers out in Brooklyn with his family, and there was never a dull moment. I stole my first car with him, got into my first bloody fist fight with him, and shot my first person with him. Some Latin nigga that was trying to rob Linx. I caught his ass from behind and hit 'im up.

Three weeks after that event, Linx got locked up for a home invasion and armed robbery. He wound up doing five years in the joint, and we kind of fell off from there. By the time he got out, I was in college and doing my own thing, and he was trying to catch up after being frozen in time for five years. In New York if a nigga was off the scene for five years, it felt more like twenty. New York was a fast-moving city. It was hard to stay on pace with anything here.

I opened the door and he stepped in smelling like Loud. "Yo, what it do, kid? I hear you need to step yo' toe into some hot shit so you can get yo' paper right. Say no mo'." He opened his arms and hugged me.

I frowned and broke our embrace quickly. "Son, watch yo' mouth. I got Lonnie sitting on the floor. She don't need to be hearing all of that nonsense." I ushered him all the way in and closed the door.

He put his fist to his mouth. "Aw, shit, my bad, kid. Where she at?" He turned and looked behind him, his long, thick dreads swinging. Linx was over six feet and slim. He was blind in one eye, and it was pure white. When he was just ten years old, his little brother had shot him in the eye with a B.B. gun, and he'd never recovered. Linx was dark-skinned. His temper was a little worse than mine.

I brushed past him and headed into the living room. "She in here. And what you talking about? You must've hollered at my mother about my situation or something?"

When I stepped into the living room, Lonnie ran over to me and wrapped her arms around my legs. I picked her and held her. I loved her so much.

"You already know me and my aunt keep a close bond, so don't worry about all that. Huh, I got this for you." He pulled out a knot of hundred dollar bills and tried to hand them to me. "That's twenty gees right there. You don't owe me nothing. I'm eating out here, son, and my blood should be eating, too."

I pushed his hand away. "You already know I don't accept no hand-outs. You can let me hit the Ave or something so I can earn my own slice, though. I can definitely use that type of scratch right there, Dunn."

He reached his hand out and tried to rub Lonnie's cheek, but I prevented that by turning my back on his ass.

"Damn, kid, what's good? Why you acting funny wit' the baby and shit?"

"Nigga, you ain't about to put yo' filthy hands on her face. You just came from outside. She breaks out real easily."

He waved me off and took a Dutch out from behind his ear, placed the money on the table, and got ready to light it. I stopped him, and this made him mad. I could tell because he mugged me for a full sixty seconds. "Damn, son, what's up?"

"Bruh, you ain't finna blow in front of her. Wait until my moms get out of the bathroom, and then we can ride or somethin'. I gotta find out how I'ma earn them twenty bands. I need that."

He put the Dutch back behind his ear and shook his head. "You ain't gotta earn it. It's already yours. But since you insisting on it, I do got a move I can use your assistance with. Let's ride for a minute." His face turned into a big smile before he stepped beside me and looked across the living room at my mother, who had just emerged from the bathroom. "Inez, wow. You look good, Aunty. I see you ain't aging at all." He closed the distance between them fast, picked her up, and twirled her around before setting her back down and kissing all over her lips and face. She laughed and acted like she was trying to fight him off, but I could tell she really wasn't putting up an honest effort. She was loving the attention.

He kissed her lips for the last time and pulled up about an ounce of Red Miami Heat. "Yo, I know you real particular about your ganja, but you gotta try this Heat from the 305. I'm telling you, it'll change your outlook on smoking outside of Puerto Rico."

My mother took the weed and sniffed the big Ziploc bag. She smiled and looked up to him. "What, cigars? How do you expect me to try this out?" She opened the Ziploc and sniffed inside of it, inhaling deeply.

"I thought you ain't use nothing but Tops?" He shrugged his shoulders. "Huh, here, I got two Dutches. I'll grab you a few more from the gas station. I need to holler at Jahmani for a little while anyway, you know, to take care of that money situation." He winked at her and smiled.

She blushed, then nodded. "Yeah, you do that. I gotta give Lonnie a bath, anyway. Come on, li'l girl." She took her from my arms and kissed my cheek. "Baby, y'all be safe out there. I'll see you later." She walked over to Linx, and he kissed her cheek as well. "Don't let nothing happen to my son, nephew. I'm serious."

***

Linx had an all-black Porsche truck with red guts. His name was stitched into the headrests of his seats. There were nine-inch television screens in the back of the car, and one seven-inch one in the sun visor in front of me. He had a five-inch one in the steering wheel as well. I could tell he was getting money, and I wanted in.

He handed me the blazing Dutch, blowing smoke past my shoulder. "Huh, kid, try this out for size."

I took five quick pulls from it back-to-back and held all the smoke in my lungs before handing it back to him. The smoke had my chest feeling like it was on fire. I slowly blew it out and broke into a fit of coughs. I felt like I'd swallowed a bunch of razor blades. My eyes were tearing up and running down my cheeks.

Linx had his console converted into a mini refrigerator. He opened it and handed me an apple juice, laughing. "Nigga, you gotta take it easy with that Miami heat. Them niggas down there in the 305 don't be jacking about that shit for nothing." He patted me on the back and shook his head.

I drank half the bottle of juice and sat back in the seat with my eyes bloodshot red. I was high as a kite. Every time I exhaled, I felt higher and higher. "Yo, what's good wit' the money? I need a move that'll make us even. I got a full plate, and it's gon' get fuller before anything else." I drank some more of the juice, killing the rest of it, and burping with my mouth closed. It felt cool and soothing going down my throat.

"I want you to sweat somethin' wit' me tonight." He looked over at me and curled his lip. He pulled away from the curb, and down the dark street of Dyse Avenue.

"When you say sweat, are you talking about bodying something?"

"Nigga, you already know I ain't make the drive all the way out to the Bronx for nothing. I got some business out here that one of the Blood bosses want me to handle. It ain't nothing major, just a few Crab niggas gotta be put down. You wanna earn that twenty bands, you'll handle this li'l shit wit' me and we'll be even." He frowned and looked out of his driver's side window before turning on to the busy street of East 174th. He rolled past Bronx Envision High School, which was my old school. I began thinking about Mardi and had to shake my head to get her off my mind. I was missing her, and hated myself for doing so. "Yo, how many cats we talking? And is there any females that gotta go down, too?" I didn't give a fuck about putting lead to a nigga, but for some reason, when it came to putting down a broad, I felt some type of way. I guess more than anything I didn't want that karma coming back to my mother, or even Lonnie. I didn't know what I would do if anything serious ever happened to either one of them.

He shrugged his shoulders. "The target is two niggas. Now, if we roll over there and it's a few bitches wit' 'em, you already know everybody gotta go. That's the law of the land. But you ain't gotta trip on that. I'll put the hot ones in the hoes' heads if need be. The niggas gotta go down, though. Everything already set in place. This hit is coming from way above my head, so I'm just following orders." He looked over at me. "You cool wit' killing up some shit tonight? It might be a few bricks in it for you, too. I mean, I know you doing the whole college thing, but you can never have too many ways of getting money. Blood an' 'em say long as the murders are carried out, all of the spoils are ours. They're projectin' for it to be a few kilos of heroin in the mix. We can't go wrong with that."

He pulled off the Dutch and tried to pass it back to me. I pushed his hand away. Now I had the bubble guts. Anytime I had to murder somebody, my stomach got to acting all crazy on me. I felt like I had to shit even though I was sure I didn't. Twenty thousand dollars was a nice piece of change. Then, if we were able to come away with a few kilos, that would sweeten the pot. I really didn't care about icing no nigga. I don't know why I felt that way, but I just did.

78

"Yo, I'm down for whatever, just let me know what the move is and how we gon' handle it. Long as we can get this shit over and done with tonight and it'll make us even, I'm good to go."

Linx laughed. "Nigga, we're already even. You don't owe me shit for that li'l chump change. I just know how you are. You don't take shit from nobody unless you can give them something of equal value in return. I respect that. I'm out here in the Bronx acting as the Reaper tonight. You saying you wanna roll wit' me, then let's handle this bitness. I got four .45s in the trunk with silencers on them and two bulletproof Kevlar vests. We gon' strap up and hit this strip club over on Hunt's Point. It's already a li'l bitch in place that got these niggas in the private room, waiting to meet their demise. We off them, hit the manager's office for them bricks, and be out. It's as simple as that. Two hours later I should be back in Brooklyn in front of the Blood bosses, ready for them to give me my official building where I'll be the head. Word is bond, it's my time, kid."

I nodded. "Then that's what it is. What these fools done done to have the bosses wanting them dead?" I asked, trying to get any type of information I could out of Linx. I felt like he was speaking in circles, and that was irritating me. I needed to know something about what I was getting into.

He shrugged his shoulders. "Don't know, and don't give a fuck. It's the life we live, kid. I'm just the Reaper. I take their lives and keep it moving. Fuck 'em." He reached between his legs and set a Tech .9 on his lap with a red bandana around the handle. "I love killing shit. I ain't changed since I was twelve." He snickered and turned up the Jadakiss coming out of the speakers in his ride while I sat back and closed my eyes.

Ghost

Chapter 8

Linx handed me two .45s. Both of them had silencers already on the ends of them and extended clips hanging out of the handles. "Yo, son, my nigga Mook gon' meet us at the back door and let us in. He one of the niggas the Heads got in place for this move. Unfortunately, I guess he into the mob for fifteen thousand, so they want me to put two in his face, as well. I fuck wit' the nigga, held his newborn a few weeks ago and everything, but it is what it is. Blood an' 'em say he gotta go, that's just what has to happen. All I want you to do is stay close by and watch my back. The strippers should just be finishing up their sets for the night, so they might be roaming around the club. Our business is upstairs. It's a elevator that'll take us to the third floor. Crab an' 'em gon' be in the platinum private rooms up that way. That's where we'll splash them at. You got me?" he asked, tossing me a white ski mask.

I took it and tucked the pistols into my waistband. "Nigga, I ain't new to this shit. You lead the way, and if I see anything out of the ordinary, I'm letting this bitch ride until it's empty." I might've sounded like I didn't have a care in the world, but on the inside I was nervous as hell. I was even letting out baby farts and shit. My stomach was bubbling up.

He parked his Porsche truck about a hundred yards from the back parking lot. "Yo, don't throw on that mask until after Mook big ass let us in. I'ma lace his bitch-ass right in the hallway, then we'll be on our way. We gotta make this shit as bloody as possible. I want the heads to know I've earned my stripes, nah mean? Let's do this." He opened the door to his truck and the interior lights came on, along with the sound of a bell indicating that the door was opened.

***

Mook opened the back door of the strip club and stepped outside of it right in front of Linx. He looked as if he stood about 6'8". He was huge, well over 300 pounds, and dark-skinned with sweat gliding down the side of his face, and a white earpiece in his right ear. He looked both ways before shaking up with Linx. "What's good, god?"

Linx shook his head and gave him half of a hug. "I'm peaceful, kid. What's the move?" He looked over his shoulder toward the parking lot. There was a group of dudes laughing to themselves as they loaded into their cars and pulled away, blasting their music.

Mook held the back door slightly ajar. "Yo, son and two of his Crab niggas up there getting extra lit. China say they been making it rain for a whole hour now. They tooting heroin and everything. Now is the best time as any to make this shit happen. That fool Icey in his office fucking his mistress, so he should be out of the picture for a li'l while. I'ma guard the hall and make sure y'all can do what you need to. The hos about to call it a night in, like, ten minutes, so I gotta make sure I steer them away from coming up there or being in that area. You know how this shit go. Who is Blood right there?" he asked, nodding wit' his head toward me.

I shook my head. "I ain't yo' concern, my nigga. You follow yo' commands and fall back," I snapped with more venom than I meant to. I just felt like his big-ass was trying to size me up. I didn't like that. I didn't give a fuck how big he was, I knew that if it came down to it, I would break his ass down into fractions if I had to.

He frowned and took a step in my direction as if he was about to come at me. "Hold on, Blood, you don't know me like that," he started.

Linx blocked his path and pushed him backward so hard

he landed with his back against the door. "Yo, that's my DNA right there, god. Fall yo' ass back. Word up." Linx looked over his shoulder at me with a snarl on his face. "Chill, kid. He good."

I nodded and knew I wanted to be the one to smoke Mook when it came down to it. "That's my bad, B. Say, Mook, I ain't mean no disrespect. Let's just handle this business and I'll buy you a bottle after it's all said and done. Cool?"

He still had an ugly mug on his face that I wanted to shoot off, but after looking down at Linx it softened, and he nodded. "Yeah, it's cool, li'l homey. Just don't let that shit happen again. Let's go." He waved for us to follow him into the hallway.

Linx leaned over into my ear before we followed behind Mook.

"Blood, we gon' smoke this nigga on the way out. Let him be on security for us first, then after it's all said and done I'ma let you have the honors. Masks on." He took his out of his waistband and slid it over his face.

I did the same and cocked my .45, my heart pounding in my chest, ready to get a move on. "I got you, cuz. Let's make it happen."

Linx disappeared into the hallway with me right behind him. Mook was already at the top of the stairs, waving us on. I could hear music coming from the club. The DJ was announcing there was only thirty minutes left before they were set to shut down for the night.

The hallway was narrow. In front of the back door was a flight of stairs that led all the way up to the third floor of the establishment, where Mook stood. Linx made his way to the top of the stairs and stopped in front of Mook. He pulled the other .45 out of his pants and held it shoulder-height. "Yo, which room are they in?"

Mook pointed. "The third door from the left, right there. The one with the yellow star on it. Come on, I'ma swipe it with this card." He jogged past Linx and stopped in front of the door he'd just pointed out to us, took the card, and swiped it through the digital lock on the side of the door. It took a second, then turned green. He pulled down on the handle and it opened a tad.

He took a step back and bumped into me all clumsy-like. His big forearm caught me on the jaw and turned my mask just enough to affect my vision out of my eyeholes. That irritated me real bad.

He turned to face me. "My bad, son. You all under me and shit, though."

Something in me snapped. I fixed my mask, took a step back, and raised the gun, pointing it right at his face before pulling the trigger. *Whoof. Whoof.* Two bullets entered his forehead and knocked his brains out of the back of his head. They splashed onto the wall behind him. He fell forward and landed in the hallway like a big tree that had been cut down. A puddle formed around his face.

Now my heart was really pounding. I was ready for the next phase. Killing him gave me just the right amount of adrenalin I needed. I stepped behind Linx. He pulled down on the handle to the private room's door, opened it. and rushed in. The music got louder the further he opened the door.

"Everybody, get the fuck down on the floor, right now!" he hollered, waving both guns around the room. I slipped in behind him with my guns out. The first thing I saw was two dude sitting with their backs to us on a couch and two strippers sitting on their laps, grinding to the music coming out of the speakers. When they heard us rush in, they dropped to the floor off of their laps.

I recognized Mach's face almost immediately. He threw

his hands in the air while his homeboy dropped to the floor on his stomach. Linx rushed Mach and smacked him with one of his guns, putting a gash in the side of his forehead. It split open and a thick glob of blood poured out of it. He fell sideways on the couch and tried to reach under it.

I peeped his move, rushed over, and slammed my knee to the side of his throat, holding it there hard enough to cause him to gag. "Bruh, he trying to grab something from under the couch!" I hollered to Linx.

Mach struggled against me. "I can't breathe! Ack! Let me up!"

I smacked him across the face with the pistol three quick times, knocking him out cold. His mouth hung wide open as the line of blood oozed out of the wound on his forehead and dripped to the carpet. I kicked his ass to the side, knelt, and grabbed the Mach .90 from under the couch. "Aw, nigga, you was looking to make a splash up in here, huh, kid?"

Linx snatched Mach's homeboy up and slammed him to the wall, placed the .45 to his temple, and leaned into his face. "Bitch-ass nigga, y'all supposed to make a late drop-off after you leave this club. I know y'all got $500,000 in cash and 15 kilos of heroin. I'ma ask you one time, whose truck is it in?"

The heavyset, dark-skinned man looked at him from the corners of his eyes, but didn't say nothing. He sniffed loudly and looked in the opposite direction of Linx.

I rushed over, aimed, and blew his kneecap off of his right leg. *Whoof!* The bullet flew out of the silencer and knocked a chunk out of him.

"Aw!" He fell to his chest and turned on his side, grabbing his knee. He landed on top of the strippers. They began to sob, covering their heads with their hands. I could see the big hole in the spot where his knee had once been.

"Awright. Awright. Fuck." He low-crawled over to the

couch and smacked his hand on top of the red leather. "It's under this couch, cuz. Take that shit. Just don't put that hot shit in me no more. Fuck, this hurts." He closed his eyes and fell to his back.

I rushed over, grabbed the very bottom of the three-person couch, and picked it up, throwing it backward to reveal three suitcases. "Cover me, bruh." I knelt down and opened the first one that was closest to me. Inside was stacks and stacks of money. I picked up one of the stacks and thumbed through it. All hundreds, blue faces. I felt like I was about to have an orgasm. Damn, I should have known Linx would have never just up and gave me twenty thousand dollars if he didn't have nearly a half million dollar sting in place. I went through the rest of the suitcases to reveal money and kilos of heroin. They were packaged in aluminum foil with Chinese writing on them. I looked over my shoulder at Linx.

He nodded his head up and down. "Hell yeah. Close them bitches. That's what we came for." He stepped over Mach's homeboy. "Fuck Crabs, nigga. It's Blood or nothing." *Whoof. Whoof. Whoof. Whoof. Whoof. Whoof. Whoof.* Fire spit out of his gun again and again. His bullets tore into Mach's guy's flesh, leaving big holes in his face and neck. His body jumped from the carpet over and over again until the shooting stopped. Then Linx took a step back and aimed his guns down at Mach. "Blood out, nigga." *Whoof. Whoof. Whoof. Whoof. Whoof.* Once again his bullets slammed into Mach's body, sending him on his way.

The strippers jumped up and ran to a corner. I could tell they were in a frenzy and on the verge of becoming hysterical. Linx, in a zone, turned his guns on them, aimed, and fired. *Whoof. Whoof. Whoof. Whoof. Whoof. Whoof.* I watched bullet after bullet fly into the strippers until they were massacred. Linx took both of his guns and put them on his waist. "Grab that merch, Blood, and let's get the fuck out of here."

I threw him two of them and grabbed the last one, heading out of the room behind him. It smelled like blood, fecal matter, and gun powder. The stench was strong enough to make me gasp for air. I took one look backward at the deadly scene before running into the hallway behind Linx. He kicked open the back door that led to the stairwell. We jumped down the stairs, rushing as fast as we could, threw open the back door that led into the parking lot, and ran across it. I could barely breathe trying to keep up with him. His long legs were moving. Mine were more muscular and heavy, but somehow, some way, I stayed on his heels until we got back to his truck and stormed away from the scene.

***

Instead of hitting up my mother's pad, we went to mine. I stayed a block over from my mother. My brownstone was directly across the street from Starlite Park on East 174th. I sat in a chair in my Den and looked up at Linx as he counted the money in front of me. He had the money in neat stacks on one side of the table, and on the other side was the money he had yet to count. It took him thirty minutes to come to a total.

"Five hundred thousand on the head. And fifteen kilos of heroin. Them niggas was holding, Blood. Gillie was right." He started to put the money back into the suitcases all neatly.

I stood up. "Yo, seeing all that scratch, that li'l twenty gees ain't shit. What's yo' cut on this?" I asked, curious. I needed more money than he'd given me. I'd been a part of five new murders and armed robbery. I knew for a fact I could pop each one of those kilos for forty thousand apiece. That was in bulk. If I dimed them up, I could make well over a hundred thousand. Twenty gees was peanuts.

He laughed. "Yo, I knew that greed would come out of yo' ass sooner or later. You seeing all this treasure, and it ain't enough for you now, huh?" He laughed and continued to pack up the suitcases.

I shook my head. "Nall, it ain't. So, what we gon' do about that?"

He snickered. "I don't know, what you looking for?" He looked over to me and curled his lip. I could see the evil in his eyes.

Linx was my cousin. We were blood. We'd been running buddies ever since we were kids, but even before our relation he was a Brooklyn nigga, and as grimy as they came. I was from the Bronx, born and bred. We didn't fuck with Brooklyn niggas because they were so cutthroat, and Linx was no different.

Now, I loved my cousin, but when it came to my scratch, I wasn't about to let nobody shit on me or treat me less than a man. I didn't give a fuck who they was or how they got down. I was a man before anything else. "Son, you already gave me twenty gees. You got five hundred right there and fifteen bricks. Give me twenty more and two of them bricks and we're good."

He ran his tongue over his gold teeth and sucked them without looking over at me. "I gotta check this merch in with the mob first. Once Blood an' 'em sign off that I got what they said was here, then I can walk away with it all. They just wanna make sure I'm one hunnit. 'Nah mean?"

"Yo, to be honest, I don't give a fuck about them. It's about me right now. I got a plate full of people to support. You lookin' real chunky right now. I gotta get mines, Blood, word up. Cut me off my piece and check the rest of that shit in with yo' Blood niggas. That shit ain't got nothing to do wit' me."

Linx flared his nostrils and scooted his chair all the way

back from the table. "So what you saying, Blood? If you don't get what you just asked for, then what?" He looked from my Jordans all the way up until his good eye was peering inside of mine.

Now my heart was pounding. "It ain't no 'if I don't get what I'm asking for' because I'ma get that or we about to light this bitch up. Nigga, ain't no way you about to walk out of here with all of that money and dope and the god don't get his full cut. Don't take our relation as a weakness of mine, because all I'm seeing right now is green. That's on my mother." I slammed my hand on the table. "Break me off my chop."

He sat looking in my eyes for two minutes, then slowly smiled. "Okay. You right. Let me give you what you got coming." He scooted up to the table and counted out twenty gees, pushed it across the table along with two bricks of heroin. "Here you go, li'l cousin. Enjoy that shit, 'cause I ain't fucking wit' you no more. That's on my Blood." He stood up and filled the suitcases, glancing over at me every now and then and laughing out loud.

None of that intimidated me. Yeah, he was a killer and all that good shit, but so was I. I had a lot of lives riding on what I did in those streets. While I appreciated him for giving me the twenty up front, there was no way I could accept less than ten percent of a murderous lick. I was a Bronx nigga. The streets taught you that all pies were supposed to be cut down the middle whenever you hit a lick with your dogs. The fact Linx was walking away with more than eighty percent of everything had me feeling like a chump. Had he not been my cousin, I would have bodied him right there and took everything. The Bronx gorilla in me was screaming for me to do it anyway.

"Son, drop me back off at my mother's building so I can make sure she straight, then you can go on about your business."

He gathered all of his things. "Nigga, fuck you. I ain't taking you nowhere. Use some of that money to call you a Uber to take you a block up. Word is bond." He sucked his teeth again and mugged me with anger in his eyes.

"Yo, so you getting in your chest because you had to break me off from your plate, kid. Really?" Now I was heated and ready to snap the fuck out. "Then get the fuck out of here, bruh, before we tear this bitch up." I opened the door to my den and took a step to the side, looking at the carpet because I didn't want to make eye contact with him. I knew it would cause me to get even more angry, and the next thing that came would be bloodshed from either him, myself, or both of us.

He laughed to himself again and made his way past me, then turned around. "Nigga, if you wasn't Inez's son, I'd leave four in your face and take my shit back."

I stepped into his face and placed my forehead against his, my nostrils flaring. "Nigga, if you wasn't my mother's nephew, I'da left you back at the strip club and drove myself to her house in yo' shit. Now, get yo' punk-ass out my crib or let's bring the Reaper here right now. Word up." I took both guns off my waistband and held them at my sides, popping them off safety.

He clenched his jaw and blinked more than usual. I could tell he was fuming. Had I been anybody else, his guns would have been out already. Even growing up as kids we fought almost every week. Once or twice a week. Some of our fights would get really bloody. We'd stay away from each other for a few days and be right back kicking it.

"In Brooklyn, niggas don't pull out they guns unless they ready to use them, or die because they didn't." He trailed his eyes down to my handguns. "What you gon' do?"

Soon as he asked that question, my doorbell rang twice,

causing us both to jump. I put one of my guns on my waist, and rushed to the front of the house, peeking out of the peephole.

Linx waited until I moved out of the way and did the same. "Aw, hell yeah. I'm finna murder this bitch." He started to undo the locks of my door in his haste, pulling his gun out of his waistband.

Ghost

Chapter 9

The door swung open, and before I could react, Linx pulled Mardi into the apartment and slung her to the floor. He stepped over her and grabbed Ari by the throat, bringing her inside of my crib. He kicked the door closed and held her up in the air against the wall with one hand.

"Bitch, I told you when I caught you, I was gon' kill you. Didn't I say that?" He squeezed harder and harder. She kicked her legs and tried to fight against his hold.

I was in shock. I didn't know what was going on. I didn't know whether to stop him or stand back and allow him to kill her. I didn't know what she'd done to cross him.

Mardi got to her feet, her eyes bucked. "Holy shit! Let her go, Linx. Come on. You're killing her," she pleaded. She rushed over to grab the arm that was choking Ari.

Linx dropped her, turned to Mardi, and smacked her so hard she flew into my arms with her mouth split. She yelped. And held onto me. This pissed me off. She fell to her knees, crying like a baby.

"Bitch, stay out of my bidness! This Crab bitch about to die. You're next if you try that shit again!" he snapped.

Ari scooted backward with tears in her eyes. "Why are you doing this? What have I done to you, Linx?" She wound up with her back against my closet door, trembling.

Linx rushed up and picked her back up, choking her against the wall. He placed the barrel of his gun to her forehead and cocked the hammer. "Bitch, you set me up for your brother to do me in. I told you that nigga should have killed me. Now you gon' pay." Spit flew out of his mouth and dripped down his chin.

"I swear to God, I didn't. I'm not that type of person. I didn't know what he had planned. Please don't kill me. I'm only nineteen," she cried.

"Nall, fuck that. Bitch, open yo' mouth. Open up!" he hollered.

She pressed her lips tighter together and moved her head around as much as she could.

"Linx, what the fuck are you doing, man? What's good wit' shorty?" I asked, getting nervous. I didn't want him killing nobody in my crib. That murder would trace back to me, there was no way around that. On top of that, Ari was the female I'd been trying to get to know. For some reason I found her so interesting. I was hoping I would cross paths with her again, but not like this. In my opinion, she'd saved me from Mach and his goons, who acted as if they were ready to waste me for talking to her. I felt one favor deserved another.

Linx pointed his gun at me. "Bitch-ass nigga, stay out of this. This between me and this thot, right here. I ain't but two seconds off your ass, anyway. Straight up." He turned back to Ari. "Bitch, open yo' muthafucking mouth or I'ma blow through your teeth. I'm giving you five seconds. Five seconds and you gon' catch all facials if you don't open your mouth," he warned.

Mardi crawled across the floor and wrapped her arms around her knees as blood spilled out of the gash in her lips. She cried and shook on the floor. I could tell she was terrified.

I was vexed. I didn't give a fuck what beef he had with this female now. Wasn't no way I was about to let this nigga come into my shit and act like he was the king, beating women and talking crazy to me like I was scared to die. Nah, fuck that. I couldn't let that pop off. I shook my head. "Nall, kid, you ain't doing that shit here. Fuck that. Let her go! You ain't doing that shit here." I made my way over to him.

He pointed his gun at me. "Nigga, on my Blood, you take one more step and I'm killing you, this bitch, and that ho on the floor. Now, try me. Yo mama gon' have a seizure and die when she find out. Now, test me, Blood." His face turned into a snarl.

"What?" I hollered, lowered my head, and rushed him with so much anger that I didn't give a fuck if he busted me or not. All I kept imagining in my head was my mother having a seizure and passing away. The image caused my eyes to water.

I closed the distance between us quick. He squeezed the trigger on his gun over and over, aiming at my face. The hammer clicked and clicked, but the gun didn't fire. I ran over to him and punched him as hard as I could right in the nose, picked him up, and dumped him on his head. *Whoom.* The impact caused the ground to vibrate. "Pussy-ass nigga. Don't you ever say nothing about my mother."

Before he could recover, I was sitting on his stomach and giving blow after blow to the face. Right. Left. Right. Left. Right. Left. Right. Left. Over and over again in a murderous zone. I remembered the hammer clicking, thankful his gun was empty or he'da left bullet holes all in my face. Bitch-nigga had tried to kill me. Right. Left. Right. Left. Right. Left. Right. Left.

Mardi rushed over and jumped on my back. "Jahmani. Stop. You're about to kill him. You're about to kill him, baby. Please, no!" she screamed, pulling on me as hard as she could.

Right. Left. Right. Left. Right. Left. Finally I stood up and looked down on him, my chest heaving up and down. My knuckles were bloodied. My vision was blurry. My blood pressure had to be through the roof.

I kicked him in the ribs. "Get yo' punk-ass up and out of my house. Now, nigga!" I grabbed him by his shirt, and picked him up, opened the front door, and pushed him into the hallway.

He fell to his knees, then struggled to use the banister to

stand up. Falling again, he repeating the whole process over.

Mardi rushed out to his aid. "I gotta get him to a hospital or you're going down for murder, Jahmani. Damn, why you do him like this?" she cried, wrapping his right arm around her neck.

I didn't give a fuck about that nigga no more. I slammed the door on both of them. My last sights were of a thick string of blood dripping from Linx's mouth and onto her white blouse.

Ari used the wall to get to her feet. She held her neck with her left hand, swallowing and gasping for air. "Thank you. You saved me. You saved me, Jahmani. I'm so sorry for how I treated you before. That was completely uncalled for." She walked over to me and stood in my face. I could tell she was vulnerable.

I was still hopped up with adrenaline, angry and in kill mode. "Don't worry about it, shorty. You're good. What the fuck did you do to make him react like that, anyway? And don't lie to me."

She shook her head. "Nothin', nothin' at all. Me and Linx went out on three dates. On the third date I invited him up for a drink just so we could kick back and chill. I didn't know he was a major Blood back then. I also didn't know my brother Mikey had been watching him all along. Anyway, long story short, after our third date Mikey and two members from his gang jumped on Linx and robbed him. They took over ten thousand dollars in cash from him and Linx's Benz truck. They beat him pretty severely. I swear I didn't know any of that was going to happen. I'm the one who took Linx to the hospital. Before he got out of my car, he told me he was going to make me pay for what they had done to him, even though I swore to him I had nothing to do with it. Today was my first day seeing him ever since that incident and, well, you see what went down. I know he's going to come for me now. He's well connected with those Bloods out of Brooklyn. They freaking honor him as if he's a god or something. I'm sure he is the one who killed my brother. If he didn't do it, then he for sure knows who did." She lowered her head and shook it. "I don't know why she brought me over here today. She said she was just going to check in with her boyfriend. I had no idea it was you or that he would be here. Man, this day can't get any worst." She took a deep breath, and looked up at me. "I owe you my life, Jahmani. He was going to kill me. I'm so sure of that. If it wasn't for you, my mother would be burying her last child. Our family still hasn't recovered from my brother's death yet. I don't think we ever will." Her eyes got misty.

I felt blood drip off of my fingers. I brought my right hand to my face and looked at it. The knuckle that belonged to my middle finger was visible. It bled profusely, then it began to hurt like crazy. "Fuck. How did I do this?" I groaned.

She took ahold of my hand and looked it over. "We gotta get this sewn up, and fast. You don't want it to get infected. Do you have a needle, maybe some thread? I could take care of it right now." She looked it over with care and concern.

I yanked my hand away from her. "Don't worry about it. I'll be alright." Those were the words that came out of my mouth, but I was in so much pain I felt like hollering at the top of my lungs. Blood was dripping from it like a runny faucet. "Look, we gotta get out of here. If I know Linx, that nigga be back. And when he come, he coming to kill up some shit. I don't know where you live or where you're from, but I'd advise you to be on point from here on out." I took my shirt off and wrapped it around my right hand. It was throbbing so had it made my eyes water.

"I'm not going nowhere until you let me either drop you off at a hospital or patch it up for you myself. I owe you my life. It's the least I can do. Now, stop being so stubborn."

I was wondering if her tune would change if she knew I had been the one who killed her brother? "Look, we can't do this shit here. Linx'll be back. I know my cousin. That nigga never could take a ass-whoopin'. He gon' come back with guns blazing, and we can't be here when he do. I mean, I can hold my own, but you're a female."

She dabbed at the blood that was coming from her split lip. "What is that supposed to mean?"

I was getting lightheaded. I leaned against the wall to steady myself. I needed to do something, and fast. I felt like I was seconds away from throwing up all over the carpet. "Look, I didn't mean nothing by it. You just need to be on your way."

I fell to one knee and closed my eyes. My head was really spinning now. I was shaking, my mouth super dry.

She knelt beside me and put my arm around her neck like Mardi had done Linx. Then she helped me to stand up. "I stay about ten blocks from here. I have a first aid kit there. I'll patch you up. You can rest for a minute, and then be on your merry way. I'm not taking no for an answer, either." She held me around the waist.

The intoxicating scent of her perfume wafted up to my nose. Even in my injured state, she called to me and placed me under her spell. The same spell she'd cast upon me at my mother's church. I just wanted to be in her presence. I wasn't ready to let her go just yet, even though I was acting like I did.

"Alright, forget it. Just take me there. Sew me up. I'll chill for a minute, then when I regain my strength, I'ma bounce. Wait a minute, do this fool know where you stay at?"

She shook her head. "Oh, hell no. After he made those threats, I moved. I couldn't roll the dice on my life. Come on, let's go."

She tried to make me walk forward, but I stayed in place. "Hold up. I gotta grab something. Pull your car around and meet me in the alley." I took my arm from around her.

She shook her head. "No! Look how woozy you are. You need that stitched up right away. Let's go."

I moved from under her. "Look, do what the fuck I say. I'll meet you in the alley. Now, hurry up," I ordered.

She stood back and mugged me. "Hey, I'll listen but you don't have to talk to me like that. Respect me just as much as I respect you. Okay?"

Her face was turned into a ball of anger. She looked so fine, staring at me the way she was. The dimples on her cheeks were prominent. I nodded my head. "A'ight, that's my bad. I gotchu. Just do like I say, though. I'll meet you out back."

I watched her rush out the front door. I locked it behind her and rushed into the den. I grabbed the suitcases and emptied them out into black garbage bags, then took the garbage bags and got on my stomach inside my bedroom, removed the grill of the heater vent, and took my time stuffing one bag in there at a time. It was a spot I'd used on multiple occasion whenever I hit a lick that was so big I needed to stash it away until I could come back to it. Since it was early September, it was still real hot in New York. The temperatures were in the high nineties. I wasn't expecting anybody to be turning the heating system on anytime soon. And even if they had, it wouldn't have affected the vents that ran through my house.

I felt like I could stash the money for a day, then I'd come back and retrieve it once I figured out what Linx was up to or what I was going to do with our caper. I didn't know if I was going to give it back to him or keep it for myself so I could take care of my mother and niece.

I took the twenty thousand that was on the table and stuffed it into my pockets, loaded my pistols, stuck them on my waist, and made my way down the back stairs to Ari's pink Lexus. She was waiting in the alley with the passenger's door open. I jogged over to it and got in. My hand killing me. "Let's go, Ari. I need you to take care of this, like, ASAP."

In response, Ari stepped on the gas and stormed out of the alley.

Chapter 10

"Ah, fuck! Why you didn't tell me the whole basin was full of alcohol?" I groaned, squeezing my eyelids tightly together. I felt like my knuckle was being pulled out of my hand by pliers. My whole right arm felt numb because of the pain the alcohol inflicted. My eyes rolled into the back of my head.

She rubbed my back. "You're fine. Had I told you what it was, you would have never put your hand in there, and I need the entire area to be clean. It's the only way we can avoid infection. Linx's blood was all over you. It's never good for two people's blood to be mixed around like that. So chill and let me do my thing."

She took my hand and ran a burgundy, tightly-woven cloth over it while she held it under the alcohol. The fluid inside the basin had turned bloody. She removed my hand and washed all of the blood away with some gauze, then laid my hand on a square of black cloth on the table. Grabbing a pre-threaded needle and surgical sewing thread out of her first aid kit, she got to work on my injured paw.

"Now, be very still. The more still you are, the better job I can do. When this heals, I don't want there to be a trace it ever existed. Okay?" She pinched my skin together and went right to work.

We were seated at her dining room table. Her apartment was small, but comfortable. Very plain. It smelled like lilacs on the inside. From what I could see, she had a living room, front room, and dining room set. Everything looked new. The pictures on her walls were of family, I guessed. I didn't see any roaches or rats, which was shocking for the area of the Bronx she lived in. Her place was only a few blocks away from the city dump. Rats in this area were ridiculous, and where they left off, the cockroaches picked up. I was impressed.

I looked her over. She looked focused and fine. I still couldn't believe how fine she actually was to me. My entire life I'd messed around with nothing but the baddest of the bad Latino chicks. I'm talking females with long, curly hair, exotic features, all different color eyes, and flawless bodies. This included Mardi. Then here was Ari, just a regular, run-of-the-mill, black female. There was nothing exotic about her, yet she had me mesmerized. I couldn't understand it. With her silky brown skin, deep dimples, and light freckles I felt like I was looking at the finest woman ever created.

"Say, who taught you how to do this, anyway?" I asked, trying to break the silence in the room.

"I'm going to nursing school right now. I want to be a nurse, like my grandmother was. I have ever since I was a little girl." She pulled the thread through my skin and tugged on it, then poked me with its tip and repeated the process. "What about you? Do you want more than the streets, or is that pretty much it for you?" She looked up at me, then went right back to working.

I cringed as the needle pricked me. "I've always wanted to be something out of the norm. Right now I'm studying law enforcement and sociology. I don't know what I'ma do with the knowledge just yet, but when I figure it all out, I know I'm going to be great." I closed my eyes, then opened them to watch her work.

"The Bible says a double-minded man should expect to receive nothing good in life or from the Kingdom. A man is not even a man until he knows what he wants, then goes out to grasp it." She stopped sewing me up to say that, then went back to working. "My brother had that bad. He had so many things he wanted to do in life, but he put the streets before all of them. Now look at where he is. It's just sad." She exhaled and shook her head. "I miss him."

I felt a twinge of guilt shoot through me. I didn't know what to say to her. I felt like a piece of shit, having been the one who killed her brother and hearing her talk about it. I really didn't know what to say. "I'm sorry for your loss. I mean, I know I told you that before, but I really, really mean it."

She shrugged her shoulders. "I'm dealing with it. Every day there is another battle, but as a woman I am dealing with it. I still got my mother and Mach. If I didn't have those two, I don't know what I would do. I've learned that in life you just have to be thankful for the blessing God delivers to you every single day and know His will for your life is never wrong. It's kind of hard to understand, but I'm getting there." She smiled. "You never responded to what I said about being a double-minded man."

"I didn't know you were looking for one."

I watched her continue to stitch me together. She sucked on her bottom lip. This caused her dimples to really pop. I wonder what it would feel like to rub her cheek. I'd bet my last dollar they were soft. Her lips were juicy. Did she know how to kiss? Could I get lost in a casual lip-lock with her? I didn't know, but I prayed that one day I would find out. This woman was doing something to me.

"Well, respond. Dang." She looked up at me and smiled.

The split in her lip made me want to track Linx's ass down and whoop him all over again. How could any man put his hands on something as precious as her?

"I don't really think I'm double-minded. It's more of me not really knowing where I want to put all of my focus into. I don't know if I could actually be a police officer. I took on that trade after, like, four of my homies out of the Bronx were murdered by dirty cops. Back then I just wanted to become a pig so I could take them out from the inside. But, when I actually started studying the things they taught their officers, it became intriguing to me. It's almost like the police were their own separate gang. I mean, they had rules and regulations that they had to follow, but they were part of a brotherhood or family. Their badge was their gang symbol, and no matter what, they stuck together through the dirt and all.

If you turned your back on one of them after becoming an officer, they'd set up what was called a blue wall. A blue wall is when all of the cops are against you. You're basically an outcast, just like you'd be if you snitched on one of your homies in the gang or committed treason. It's just crazy. I don't know, but I've been on the other side of the fence for so long. I just can't imagine what me being a police looks like."

"Okay, then what about a sociology? What made you study that in school?" She picked up the bottle of rubbing alcohol and turned it upside down on the cloth before wiping some of my blood away from the back of my hand. Then she went right on back to sewing me up.

I shrugged my shoulders. "I like to study facts and statistics. Our people have been screwed up ever since I've been alive, and even before me. It seems that nobody can figure out why we're at the bottom of the barrel. Well, I want to be the person who does. My plan is to reverse the curse we're under. I feel like we're the strongest and most intelligent on earth, yet as a people we are the weakest and most broken. We are under what I like to refer to as the Elephant and Chain Effect." I winced and almost yanked my hand away from her when I felt the needle poke my bone. "Fuck."

"Oh, I'm sorry. I envisioned a big elephant, and it reminded me of the last time me and my brother went to the circus as kids. I won't make that mistake again. Please, go on. What do you mean? What is the Elephant and Chain Effect?"

"Well, like you said, you've seen elephants at the circus,

and more than likely during the half time they allow children to ride on the backs of the elephants. Now, more often than not, those elephants were trained to believe they were less powerful than they really were. Back on the elephant farms, and even the zoo if you looked close enough, you'd see they got these huge elephants with these little chains around their ankles. The chains are connected to nothing more than a stump in the ground. A little, bitty piece of wood that even the trainer could walk up to and pull out of the ground at any given time. Yet here is this huge elephant that weighs more than a thousand pounds. It doesn't even think it is physically capable of freeing itself from the small chain and stump, not knowing that with one jerk it could not only break away from the chain, but it could free itself."

I watched her pull the last bit of thread through my skin, tie it in a knot, and clip it with her surgical scissors. "There, you should be good as new in a week." She gathered the scraps and tossed them in the garbage. I couldn't keep my eyes from going down and peeping her ass that was poking out of her Fendi jeans. Each step she took caused her cheeks to jiggle. I was once again mesmerized.

"So what are you saying? I mean, I think I get it, but just expound for me a little bit."

I had to snap out of my zone. I was imagining how it would feel to hit her thick ass from the back. I knew my bronze skin clappin' into her brown skin would look so good. I wondered how she sounded when she moaned? Was she aggressive, or more submissive? Did she know how to work all of that body, or was it just for show like most of the females I'd come across in the Bronx?

"What I'm saying is our people are a hundred times more strong than we actually believe we are, but the world has embedded a sense of weakness in us. It tells us we can do this or that, but when it comes to us rising up and freeing ourselves from the cycle of destruction, we feel we as a people are incapable of doing such. So many excuses come to the forefront of our minds. Valid ones, albeit, but excuses nonetheless. I guess I just wanna find the root and help our people climb out of the abyss of self-destruction. I don't know how I'm going to do it, but I am one day. It's my dream. That and buying my mother her own house. She deserves it." I took a deep breath and imagined the face of my mother standing in front of a home I'd just bought her. Man, I couldn't wait.

Ari stopped cleaning up the table to stare at me. She shook her head. "I swear, you can't judge a book by its cover. I would have never guessed any of those things went through your head. I honestly thought you were just a street dude, just one of those regular, everyday, run-of-the-mill Bronx Trap Stars with no goals, no ambitions outside of the drug game, and ultimately no future. It's nice to know there is more to you than just a bad temper and a handsome face." She smiled.

I don't know if I was blushing or not. Man, I hope I wasn't, but her li'l comments had me feeling some type of way. I was trying me best to not let that be known. I put a frown on my face and waved her off. "How do you know Mardi?" My stomach growled. I needed to get some food. I was hungry as a lion.

She gathered up all of the first aid kit items and held them in her arms. "We go to the same modeling agency. She's cool. She's been a sort of mentor every since I signed with them. We kick it once or twice every week, though I wish today wouldn't have been one of them. How long have you two been seeing each other? You're all she talks about. Hold on." She disappeared.

I stood there, offended. I couldn't believe Mardi had told her we were together. That wasn't the truth. I felt like she'd hated on me or something. I wasn't trying to tick off my chances of getting with Ari. There was something about her I needed. I sat in my seat, steaming. I felt like slapping the shit out of Mardi, and I didn't know why.

Ari stepped back into the room. "Hey, I know you said you were going to be on your way after I stitched you up, but whatta you say I cook us a nice, hot meal. We can talk a little more, and then we can part ways. I think I want to pick your brain a little more. I've never run across a thug with some sort of sense in his head. It's fascinating."

My stomach rumbled. I placed my hand on it. "Yo, that sounds real good. What can you cook?"

She smiled. "Do you want some fried chicken, white rice, pinto beans, and cornbread? I could whip that up in a few hours and we'd be good to go. I'm a Baltimore girl. We start cooking at nine years old."

I nodded. "That sound like a plan. You g'on in there and do your thing. I'ma check in with my mother to make sure she's good."

She turned around and left the living room. Once again, my eyes trailed down to that fat booty. She left the scent of her perfume behind, and that had me harder than a brick. I sniffed the air and shook my head, pulled out my phone, and called my mother.

***

Ari handed me the bottle of Tabasco sauce. I took off the top and drenched my three pieces of chicken. I had two breasts and a leg, and I was about to do some major damage. I'd already tried out her rice and beans, and they were good. After drenching my chicken, I slid my bottle across the table. "Let's eat!" I slapped my hands together, geeked. The sounds of

Alicia Keys crooned out of the speakers.

Ari looked across the table at me and smiled. "You're so funny."

I picked up that drumstick and tore into it with my teeth like a barbarian. It was so hot I dropped it back to my plate, but not before getting a chunk of meat with my teeth. I started chewing it and trying to blow on it at the same time. Man, it was so good. Or I was just hungry. Either way, I was getting it on.

She spooned up some of her rice after sprinkling some sugar on it. I looked at her like she was crazy. She caught me and frowned. "What? Why are you looking at me like that?"

"Because I never seen nobody put sugar on their rice before."

"Well, it's good. Maybe you should try it."

She smiled, showcasing her deep dimples and a twinkle in her eye. I would have tried anything she wanted me to. Damn, she was fine.

"Huh, just get a spoonful of rice and let me put a pinch on it. I bet you'll like it. And if you don't, you can always spit it out. How about it? She took a teaspoon of sugar and pinched it, ready to put it over my rice.

I didn't know if I was gon' like it or not, but just knowing the sugar was coming from her fingers was enough to make me give it a shot. "G'on 'head, let me try it out." I moved my plate closer to her.

She took my spoon, scooped some of the rice from my plate, and put the sugar on it, then held it out for me. "Huh, try this."

My eyes locked onto her brown ones as I allowed her to feed it to me. I chewed with my eyes closed remembering her beautiful face. Even with the split in her lip, she looked good to me. I don't know why I had never dated a black sista before.

I mean, Mardi was dark enough, but she was Puerto Rican. I wanted Ari.

I chewed and could not believe how good it tasted. The rice coupled with the butter and the hint of sugar was a perfect blend. I couldn't deny that. "Damn, I gotta keep it one hunnit, this is good, shorty. You might be onto something."

She placed the spoon back on my plate, grabbed a napkin, and wiped my mouth. "My name is Ari, not shorty. And I'm glad you like it. Would you like me to add some sugar to the rest of the rice that is on your plate?" She looked into my eyes almost challenging-like.

I nodded my head. "Yeah, that'd be cool. Oh, and thank you, too."

She took a bit of the pure cane sugar and sprinkled it onto my rice, mixing it up for me and everything. "Thank me for what? It's just sugar. Everybody does this in Baltimore."

Her scent kept coming across the table and right up my nose. She smelled so good. I found myself inhaling before I had completely exhaled all of the way. "I'm not just talking about the whole sugar ordeal. I'm thanking you for stitching me up, for inviting me into your crib, and for cooking me this meal. You ain't have to do none of this, but you did. That means a lot to me. I'm fo' real." I reached across the table and touched her little hand. It was warm, but then she pulled it back.

She lowered her head and smiled. "Well, you're welcome. But if we're going to start thanking each other, then I gotta thank you for saving my life. It took a lot of guts to stand up to a man waving around two guns like a maniac. I'm positive that had you not stepped in, he would have killed me with no remorse. His record is well known. So, if anybody should be thanking somebody, it should be me thanking you. I still can't believe you stepped in. I mean, especially after how rude I was to you." She looked up to me and smiled weakly. "I'm sorry about that. I just thought you trying to pick me up at church was a little tacky." She picked up her chicken and bit off of it, chewing while looking into my eyes.

Now I lowered my head and blew air out of my jaws. Man, I didn't understand how this li'l broad was getting to me like she was. I'd fucked with plenty of bad chicks, and it wasn't like I was an ugly nigga or nothing. Nall, from what I understood from most women, I was a handsome man. Light caramel skin, physically fit, naturally wavy and curly hair I'd picked up from my Puerto Rican side of the family. I always made sure to dress nice and I was strapped in the basement, so I didn't have any insecurities other than my high blood pressure. But for some reason Ari was taking me through it. She had me feeling some type of way. Every time she looked into my eyes, I got weak. That was starting to bother me a little bit.

"So, Ari, I don't mean to get into your business or anything, but which one of these dudes around here got you locked down? I know you gotta be talking to somebody. I mean, you're way too bad not to be."

She raised her eyebrow. "Is that the best you got?" She snickered and took a sip from her glass of Hawaiian punch.

I shifted uncomfortably in my seat. I spooned up some of the rice and ate it. Man, it was so good. I broke off a piece of the cornbread and crushed it up over my pinto beans before picking up one of the breasts. I didn't know what to say next to her, so I figured keeping my mouth stuffed with food would create a diversion.

Ari put her chicken down and wiped her fingers on a piece of paper towel. "No man can ever lock me down. I am a queen. My temple belongs to God first, and then the man I marry. There is no way I would ever allow myself to be conquered by any of these men in this neighborhood. Majority of them don't have any realistic goals, dreams, or the ambition to bring them into fruition. It seems everybody out there is looking to take shortcuts that will give them short-term happiness and a long-term life of pain. I want more for myself. I think I have something to offer to the world. I just don't know what it is yet, but I'm searching. But, to answer your question, nobody has me locked down. I am free. Why do you ask?" She gave me a knowing glance before drinking more of her juice.

After hearing all of that, I definitely felt like my legs were stripped from under me. I felt like my tongue had been pulled out of my head. My brain was spinning too fast, and I didn't know what else to say. A part of me was irritated. I was trying to find something about her physically that I didn't like. I needed to focus on a weakness of hers, that way the infatuation I was experiencing would hopefully die. I shrugged my shoulders. "Oh, no reason. Just curious, that's all."

There was a pounding on her front door. I jumped out of my seat and pulled my pistol off my waist, cocking it with my good hand, ready to splash something. I knew that nigga Linx would be back. I just wasn't expecting him so soon. "Yo, I thought you said he didn't know where you stayed?" I finished chewing the chicken that was in my mouth, swallowing it.

She stood up with her eyes bucked, wiped her mouth with a paper towel, and handed me one. "He doesn't. There is no way it's him. Unless Mardi has shown him where I live."

She held up one finger, and made her way toward the front door. "Hold on." She stepped up to the door, looked through the peephole, and took a deep breath.

Ghost

Chapter 11

Mardi stormed through the door. She shook her head from side to side and brushed past Ari, headed in my direction. "How could you do that to him, Jahmani? You fucked that boy up. He lost so much blood that I don't know what's going to happen to him. Are you crazy or something?" She ran her fingers through her long hair and licked her juicy lips. I could see the sweat along the edges of her forehead. It caused the baby hairs to wave up. She smelled like Fendi perfume and sweat. One of the nails on her right hand had been broken. The other nine were French tipped with the Fendi logo all over them.

"Son was about to kill all of our asses, and you're over here speaking like I was in the wrong? Really?" I waved her off and stepped back into the dining room, ready to finish my food before it got cold. Ari had did her thing with it. I wanted to enjoy it. Besides, I was still hungry, and in my book Mardi wasn't talking about shit.

Had it been up to me and they hadn't been there, I would have put two bullets in Linx's face and left it at that. That punk had tried to waste me. Had he any bullets left, he would have. I didn't understand how Mardi didn't peep that, but I was too irritated to explain it to her. I picked up my chicken and got to attacking it again, spooning some of the rice into my mouth with the beans and corn bread mixed.

Mardi stepped into the dining room and stood behind my chair. "Baby, what are we going to do? Linx kept saying as soon as they let him out of the hospital, he's going to kill you and her. I swear I believe him. You know he get down. So, what are we going to do?"

She placed her hand on my shoulder, then started to rub the back of my neck like she normally did. It was something I had fallen in love with, and usually when I was angry it could calm me down and put me in a cool space, but for some reason all I could think about was murder. I wanted to murder Linx. I knew he didn't make threats he didn't intend on standing on. If he was saying that he was going to kill me and Ari, then he honestly meant to. That had my blood boiling.

I looked up to her and scoffed. "Fuck you keep saying 'what are we going to do' for? He ain't say your name, so you're good. The only people that should be worried about what he's going to do is me and her." I nodded my head at Ari. She stood a safe distance away, looking on with her eyes wide open.

"Look, I'm about to call my cousin Mach. I ain't about to let nobody just up and kill me without doing nothing about it. I'm scared. I wish you would have never brought me over there today, Mardi. Damn, I wish you wouldn't have. Now I gotta worry about this for God knows how long. I was sure he'd forgotten all about me. If y'all would excuse me." She left out of the room, headed toward the back of the house where she stepped into her bedroom and closed the door.

As soon as she did, the scent of Mardi filled the room. Mardi knelt beside me and rubbed her hands over my thighs. "*Papi*, are you mad at me?" she asked, looking up at me.

I shook my head. "Nall, I ain't mad at you. Why would I be, Mardi?" I continued to eat my foot, even though my appetite was fast leaving me. I had murder on my mind. I had to get to Linx before he got at me. I knew that fool was an animal off the leash. If I didn't make it to him before he made it to me, things would look real grim. I didn't know what he had up his sleeve. I knew he didn't like taking no L's.

"Baby, let's get out of here and go to my place. Or maybe even a hotel or something until all of this blows over. I mean, y'all are family, right? He wouldn't really try to kill you for real, would he?" She started to bite on one of her manicured nails, sweat peppered along her brow.

I slammed my hand on the table. "Yo, fuck that nigga, ma. Word is bond! That fuck-nigga can't do shit to me that I can't do to him. That punk bleed just like I do. Far as I'm concerned, I should have knocked his head off back at my crib. That way you wouldn't've had to rush his bitch-ass to the hospital all concerned and shit. You would have made sure I was good and stayed by my side like you were supposed to." I curled my upper lip, the jealousy of the situation obviously coming out of me.

Mardi covered her mouth with her right hand. "Oh my God. Baby, I didn't even look at it like that. I didn't want him to die. Had I not got him to the hospital when I did, that boy would have bled out. I'm sure of it." She laid her face on my lap. "So, then, you are upset with me?"

Ari rushed out of her bedroom with tears streaming down her face. She fell to her knees in the dining room and shook her head. "Not again. Not again. Oh my God, not again!" she screamed and broke into a fit of sobs.

I scooted my chair all the way back and got on the floor, wrapping her into my arms. "What's the matter, Ari? What happened?"

She turned and put her face in my chest, crying her heart out. I could smell her hair care products clearly. The heat radiating off of her body seemed to warm my soul. The longer she cried, I felt like a part of me was being wounded. It made me angry.

She grabbed my shirt in her fist and balled it up. "My cousin. Oh my God, my cousin Mach. My aunt says they just found him dead in some strip club over on Hunts Point. I was just talking to him yesterday. How did this happen?" She sobbed and buried her face in my chest again.

I held her tighter and felt sick on the stomach. I didn't

know what to say. I knew I had a hand in her cousin's death. I felt like a straight sucker for consoling her, but at the same time I didn't want to let her go. She felt so good in my arms. I continued to hold her, speechless.

Mardi looked down on us with a frown on her face. She grabbed Ari's arm and pulled her to her feet. "Come here, girl." Once she was on her feet, she hugged her. "Shouldn't you be there for his mother while she's going through this tough time?" Mardi asked, looking down to me.

Ari slowly nodded her head. "You're right. I should be, because I know she needs me." She unlocked her arms from around Mardi and rushed into her bedroom, grabbed her car keys, and came back, slipping her left foot into a pair of pink and gray Airmax.

"Look, I should be gone for a few hours. The both of you are more than welcome to stay in the guest room down the hall and to the left. The bed is already made, and there are some clean towels and linen in the closet right next to the bathroom. Food in the kitchen. Help yourself, just clean up afterward. I gotta go." She rushed out of the door and slammed it behind her. I could hear the key turning in the lock, then her feet running down the stairs.

Mardi stepped into the front room, checked the locks on the door, and came back into the dining room with a frown on her face. "You're consoling that bitch? Really?" she snapped, stepping in front of me.

I stood up. "What?"

"You heard me. I ain't never seen you wrap your arms around a bitch just because she was crying, especially not in my presence. You got a thing for her black ass, don't you?"

I tried to side-step her, but she blocked my path again. "Yo, get out of my face, shorty. You know I don't like that shit." I held out my forearm, my temper already beginning to rise.

She brushed it away. "Look, Jahmani, I don't care what you're talking about. This bitch done cooked for you, got you all up in her house. I caught the way you were looking at her more than once. Then, as soon as she come in here crying, you damn near broke your neck to console her. You ain't never acted like that with nobody other than me, and that's been so long I forgot what it feels like. Dang." She shook her head. "Why her, though. What the fuck does she have on me? Is it because I took Linx to the hospital and she stayed with you?"

"Shorty, you're jumping the gun. I saw her crying, and I just wanted to make sure she was good. That's it, that's all. Besides, you ain't my woman. I'm free to feel whoever I wanna feel." I grabbed my plate and took it to the garbage, dumping the food off into the can. I washed the plate, along with my cup after I downed the juice in it. I was hoping Ari was okay. I should have went with her. Damn, I should have.

Wrinkles appeared across Mardi's forehead as she looked up at me, shaking her head. "That's what you gon' come at me with, huh? You can't even be man enough to let me know how you're really feeling about that girl? Wow. How fucking immature can you be?"

I ignored her, but she reached past me and knocked the plate out of my hand and into the sink. It shattered. Pieces of glass popped into the air, one of them hitting me on the bottom of my chin. Now I was vexed.

"Nigga, talk to me! Damn!" she screamed.

I turned to my right, grabbed her by the neck, and pinned her against the wall of that kitchen. She brought both of her hands up to try to peel my one away from her neck, but I wasn't about to let her go just yet. My head was pounding. My vision was hazy because I was so mad. Sometimes she really got under my skin. I didn't feel like going there with her right then. "Mardi, I done told you about playing so fucking much. I don't know what yo' problem is, but you better get yo' shit together, and fast. Word is bond." I pushed on her neck and let her go, turnin' my back on her. I walked to the sink and began to pick up the shards of glass, dumping them into the garbage can.

She stood a safe distance away, holding her neck. "No, the fuck you didn't, Jahmani. No, you didn't just choke me." She kicked her wedges off of her pretty feet. "You got me fucked up."

She rushed over to me and grabbed the back of my shirt, pulling. I could feel her nails going into my skin. "I told you about putting your hands on me. I ain't one of these average hos out here in the Bronx." She punched me in the back of the head, then wrapped her arm around my neck, trying to pull me down to the ground. "I hate you! I hate you!" she hollered.

I did everything I could to catch my balance, but still wound up falling to one knee before I slipped out of her grasp. I scooped her li'l ass up and slammed her to the floor. I held both of her wrists out at her sides, right above her shoulders. "What the fuck is your problem, Mardi? You acting like a little-ass girl right now. You keep playing wit' me, I'ma fuck you up."

She kept on moving this way and that, kicking her legs until finally I straddled her and continued to hold her down. She was making me more and more mad. She wrapped her legs around me and squeezed as hard as she could. I guessed she was trying to crush my ribs or something. Her dress skirt moved backward to her waist.

She grunted, "Get off of me, Jahmani. I swear to God, I hate you. You just gon' keep on holding that Puerto Rico shit over my head for the rest of my life, ain't you?"

She humped upward to try to buck me off of her. My

crotch was situated right on her middle, so every time she bucked or humped, it didn't do nothing but smash my piece. After a while it started to feel kind of good. I couldn't lie about that. Plus, her skirt dress was all the way around her waist now. I could make out the cameltoe in her panties. The lace was hugging her mound so tight it was like a second skin. My dick became harder and harder.

"Yo, just chill, Mardi. You making me feel some type of way."

She laid still for a second, then raised her head to look up at me. I still had ahold of her wrists. "What?" Her forehead was covered in sweat.

My dick throbbed in my pants. "Let's just get up and talk about this, a'ight?" I let one of her wrists go. She took it and smacked me across the face with it so hard my head turned to the right. My neck popped.

"Let me go, nigga. I'm tired of yo' shit. Fuck this." She humped up from the kitchen floor and ground into me. Her pussy-packed panties ground into the denim of my pants.

"Oh yeah! A'ight, I see what you on." I yanked her panties to the side with so much force I ripped the material. Her brown sex lips came on display. They looked slightly open and engorged. I reached between us and undid my pants, pulling them open and yanking my dick out. "I'm finna fuck the shit out of you. That's on my mother. I know what you looking for." I placed the head to her hole and tried to get him inside of her opening.

She twisted her hips this way and that. "Get off of me, Jahmani. No! I ain't going there with you no more. Since you want that bitch so bad, have her give you some pussy." She beat at my chest and struggled to get from under me.

I leaned down and bit into her neck. "Shut yo' ass up. You finna give me some of this pussy. That's what you was angling for, right?" I found the opening between her lips and slammed my dick into her as hard and as deep as I could. I could hear the sound of it as it forced its way into her small hole greased with her juices. She felt hot and velvety.

"Aw! *Papi*! What the fuck?" She arched her back and closed her eyes. She wrapped her legs around my lower back, and crossed her ankles. Her nails dug into my back. "Uh. Uh. *Papi*. Fuck. Fuck. *Papi*. Fuck. Me. Fuck. Me. Aw. You. So. Fucking. Deep. Shit!"

I rolled my back and sliced in and out of her pussy. My helmet burrowed its way through her tunnel, hit her bottom, then pulled all the way back only to slam its way home again. Her juices poured out of her. "I knew this was what you wanted. I knew it. You need *papi*'s dick! Ain't that right? Admit it. You love *papi*!"

I sped up my pace, and pulled her dress skirt all the way up so I could expose them big titties. Her bra came into view. Her nipples poking through, heavily engorged. I sucked them through the material and trailed my tongue in circles all around the areolas. I could feel the bumps. It drove me crazy.

"You're taking my pussy! You're taking my pussy! Aw, *papi*! You're taking this pussy so hard. Shit!" She drug her nails all across my back, pulled her bra over her breasts, and squeezed them together. She pulled the nipple and shivered. "I'm cumming. I'm cumming, *papi*! Aw, shit! I'm cumming on this big-ass dick!" She rose up and licked my neck, then fell backward, screaming and shaking like crazy.

I dug my fingers into her thighs, pounding that pussy. I was trying to touch her ribcage. I moved her hands out of the way and nursed at her big titties, pulled at the nipples with my teeth, and sucked the areolas hard, leaving traces of spit and teeth marks all over them before laying my cheek against her right hard nipple. It poked me in the jaw and felt so good.

I closed my eyes, and Ari's face came into my mind. First her fine-ass face, and then her body. That ass. The way it jiggled when she walked. I imagined fucking her from the back with her bouncing back into me, begging for more.

I flipped Mardi onto her knees and stuck her face in the floor, grabbed a handful of her curly hair, and slid back in. I sucked my middle finger and wormed it into her anus along with my index finger.

She threw her head back. "Get out of there, *papi*. Get your fucking fingers out of my ass. Please. I can't take it. It's too much."

I slammed forward, pulled back, and did it again. Her ass jiggled. Her thighs shook. Some of her juices dripped onto the kitchen floor, then she was creating a puddle right where our sexes worked on each other. The scent of her pussy rose to my nose. It mixed with her perfume for an intoxicating blend. Her sex walls massaged me from the inside.

"Shut up, *mami*, and take this dick. Let yo' *papi* fuck this pussy like I'm supposed to." *Bam. Bam. Bam.* I slid in and out of her while my fingers played in that fat ass. I was on the brink of cumming in that wet pussy.

She slammed backward harder and harder. "Uh-huh! Uh-huh! *Papi*! Take it! Take it! Aw, fuck! Take it. Mami cumming! I'm cumming, *papi*! Aw, shit!" She slammed back into me, raised her face to the ceiling, and started to scream again.

I had my hands resting on that big ass, letting her do all the work. She popped her ass in my lap like a stripper. My eyes rolled into the back of my head, and then I was cumming so hard I couldn't breathe. I fell over her booty, still humping.

We wound up on the floor with me still connected to her, sawing in and out of her body while my seed shot out of me and into her sucking womb.

***

After I showered and threw back on the same clothes, I felt guilty about what had transpired between us mostly because ninety percent of the session I was imagining I was fucking Ari, not Mardi. I felt like I was some kind of a pervert or something. I couldn't get Ari off of my mind, no matter how hard I was trying to. I was hoping she'd text Mardi soon so I could know she was okay. I still felt weird feeling the way I did about her because I barely knew her, but I could not help what was going on inside of me. I couldn't deny it, either. I felt how I felt.

Mardi came into the room drying her long hair with a drying towel. She looked so fucking sexy in just her pink lace bra and no panties. Her brown legs were chubby. Her thick thighs had a few stretch marks going across them that made her look that much badder to me. One of the reason I hated jumping up and down between her legs was because I always walked away with some sort of renewed feelings for her. This time was no different.

She dropped the towel and climbed into the bed wit' me, snuggling all up under me. She smelled Zest-fully clean. I wrapped my arm around her and kissed her forehead. "What's good, shorty?"

She opened her thighs, and I caught another peek of her chubby gap. Her inner lips hung slightly past her outer ones. She had one of those unique pussies that I loved to suck on. The liquid that came out of it tasted good to me, too. Her pussy had been the only one I'd ever eaten, and I'd grown in love with its taste. I felt like I could eat her all day long and never get tired of it.

"Baby, I really think we need to leave the Bronx for a

while. I got some gigs coming up in Miami. Why can't we go down there for a month or so? You know, until everything calms down?"

Damn, I didn't wanna hear nothing else about her fears and all that shit. I just wanted to lay back and think about Ari and my next move. I felt like she was starting to make it seem like I should have been scared of Linx. Like I didn't get down like he did or something. That clouded my judgment and put me on the defense. "Yo, I ain't running for no nigga. Fuck that fool. If he talking like he want that sauce, then I'ma bring that shit to him first. Word is bond."

I slid out of the bed and started to get dressed when my phone vibrated on the dresser of the guest room. I rushed over and looked at the face. Samantha's picture popped up, so I answered the call, wondering why she hadn't sent me a simple text or something. "Yo, what's good, shorty? Why you calling my phone?"

I looked over at Mardi. She lowered her head and shook it from side to side. She had one foot placed flat on the bed. Her thighs were parted. She exposed her gap, and the sight of it sent tingles down my spine. I needed to hit that thang one more time, then I would be good. Man, she was like an unwanted addiction.

"Jahmani, I need you. They gon' kill me. Can you please come pick me up? I'm on East 120th, inside Lacy's Laundromat."

I took the phone off of my ear and mugged it, then put it back there. "What the fuck have you gotten yourself into?" I snapped.

"Please, let's not do this over the phone. You're the only person I can turn to. Can you please hurry? It's a matter of life and death." Her voice quivered.

"Fuck, Samantha. It's always something with you. Damn,

just chill. I'll be there in a minute." I ended the call and took a deep breath, my blood pressure rising like crazy. I felt dizzy.

Chapter 12

When I pulled up, Samantha rushed out of the laundromat with a black hoodie pulled over her head and a book bag over her right shoulder. She slid into my passenger seat and slammed the door. The sun was just starting to set. She smelled like onions and cigarettes. Both scents made my stomach turn.

"Thank you for coming, Jahmani. You ain't gon' believe what happened to me." She looked over her shoulder out the back window, then both ways, and clasped her fingers in her lap. I could tell she was worried or hopped up on drugs. I didn't know which for sure, but something wasn't right.

She opened the book bag and reached inside of it, then handed me a roll of hundreds. "Huh, this is for coming, and everything else I owe you from over the last few months while you've stepped up for Pacho. I really appreciate you doing the things you have, because you really didn't have to. You're a real nigga in every sense of the word. The only Bronx nigga I respect, that's on my daughter." She kissed me on the cheek.

I pulled off into traffic. The scratches on my back beginning to sting. Fuck, I hated when Mardi dug her claws into me. The pussy was good, but fuck, the aftermath always hurt. "Yo, where you get these chips from, goddess? Don't lie to me, either."

She looked both ways and slid down in her seat. "The less you know, the better, Jahmani. I ain't tryin' to get you involved in no bullshit, word up. Why you just can't accept this money and let that be that?" She pulled her hood further over her face and slid lower in the seat.

"Because I care about yo' silly ass. Now, tell me what's good?" I tossed the money onto her lap. I didn't want it, nor did I need it. I couldn't ever see myself taking a crumb from her, knowing she was my niece's mother. Every cent she came up with should have went toward bettering herself for my niece or getting something Lonnie needed. Only a bum-nigga would have accepted that money. Besides, I was five hundred thousand to the good, plus some change. I'd already made my mind up that I wasn't giving that nigga Linx back shit. He was already talking about murdering me, so I was gon' make him stand on that shit. it was what it was. I was all for the beef shit. Wasn't no vegetarian in me.

Samantha blew air out of her jaws and closed her eyes. "I know it's gon' be hard to believe, but I just smoked Chase and took all of this merch. He raped me twice last night at the Hilton, and I tried to fight him off, but couldn't. After we left the hotel, he made a run out to Jersey. I guess to pick up this merch I'm carrying now. Well, before we made it back here to New York, he decided to pull over by the George Washington Bridge. You know, in Heroin Alley. Long story short, do you remember that gun you saw on my dresser a li'l while back?"

I nodded. "Yeah, what about it?"

"Well, I had it in my purse all along. So, before he could snatch me up and have his way with me, I popped him twice in the chest. He dies on the spot, and I took this here merch. I didn't know what else to do." She swallowed and looked up at me.

I waited until I pulled up to a red light and grabbed the book bag from her, opened it, and looked inside. The book bag was filled with rolls of money and what looked like two kilos of cocaine. Way down in the bag was a nine millimeter and two clips. I looked down at her, shocked, then zipped the bag back and handed it to her. "Shid, look like you hit one hell of a lick to me. Why are you all paranoid and shit?" I pulled off at the green light and got onto the expressway.

Once there, she sat up in her seat and pulled the seatbelt around her body. "Because them Dyse Ave Crip niggas know

126

I rolled out with him. I was supposed to be the driver. The transporter. When they find out he got stanked and nothing happened to me, they are going to be suspicious. After the suspicion comes the drama. Drama I can't afford to have. I ain't about that life like that. I mean, I'll bust my gun if I have to, but that's about it. Then, on top of that, I have Lonnie to think about. They know where we stay. It's dangerous all around the board."

Now she had my attention. I didn't know that they knew where she laid her head, but of course they would. Samantha didn't know she was never supposed to shit where she laid her head. Or, in other words, a nigga was never supposed to do dirt from out of his home. One of the cardinal rules of the game was always do business away from where family rested. The game had a way of coming back to settle the score, no matter what had been done. A nigga was never supposed to let anybody know where he laid his head, or those that he loved laid theirs.

"Yo, well, we gon' go ahead and pick her up right now. That way we ain't gotta worry about nothing like that."

Samantha shook her head. "No! We can't. They don't even know he's dead right now. After I killed him, I pushed the car into the Hudson. Let me regroup and get my story together, find a nice li'l place to bring Lonnie to, and then we can go get her. But right now I am beat. I'ma have you drop me off at my mother's crib in Harlem. I'ma sleep for a few hours after I holler at Beans. That cool?"

I shrugged my shoulders. "Shorty, if that's what you wanna do, then I guess that's what it is. Just make sure Lonnie is good before it's all said and done. Nah mean? Don't have me spank that ass again." I looked over at her and smiled.

She yawned and covered her mouth with her balled fist. Her eyes were watery. "Jahmani, if you ever spank me again,

I swear to God we're fucking. That shit turn me on way too much. I already got a thing for you, so your best bet is to stay away from my lower region, period. Word up." She laid her head on her shoulder. "You remember where my mother stay?"

I nodded. "Yeah, right down the street from Marcus Garvey park. I been there a few times with Pacho." Damn, I had to get in touch with my brother. I hadn't reached out to him in a month or so. That was foul. The last time I'd reached for him, I'd put five thousand on his books. That was two months ago. Hopefully he was still good, but I didn't know for sure.

By the time I pulled up in front of Samantha's mother's crib, she was out like a light. I had to tap her on the shoulder. She stretched her arms above her head and yawned again.

"Damn, that was fast. Thank you for coming to get me, Jahmani. I don't care what you say, I know you love me. You're always the first person to come to my rescue. Your brother never got down like that. I don't know what it is about me, but you do care, and that makes me feel good." She kissed my cheek and smiled. "I'll get up with you tomorrow. I love you, li'l bro. That's my word." She stepped out and closed the door.

She couldn't have been more than five steps away from my car when I rolled down the window. "Yo, Sammy?"

She stopped and turned around. She was halfway up her mother's stoop. "What's good, kid?"

"Say, why don't you take, like, ten of them bands and hit up Pacho's books with it? I'ma hit son, too, but we always gotta make sure we're reaching for him when we got it, nah mean?"

She nodded. "Yeah, I guess you're right. I'll make sure I do that." She climbed three steps and paused, turning back around. "Nall, I can't lie to you, Jahmani. I ain't fucking wit' him like that. When son was out here, he ain't go above and beyond to take care of me and his daughter. Now that he in there, I'm just supposed to break my neck to make sure he's good? Nah! If it ain't about Lonnie, then I don't care. I mean, I wanted to reach for you because you're a real nigga, but I wouldn't even let Pacho kiss my ass no more. This is blood money, son. I'ma use this to get ahead. I'd be foolish not to. Later." She jogged up the stairs and never looked back.

I guess, on the one hand, I had to honor and respect where she was coming from. I knew my brother was a street nigga. He'd put the hood before her and Lonnie damn near every day. Ever since Lonnie had been born, I'd been making sure she was always well taken care of. Lonnie and Samantha. My brother often told me he took care of his daughter, but I couldn't confirm or deny if he did or not. That never stopped me from doing what I saw needed to be done. Lonnie was my heart, my princess, and as long as I was living, she would always be well taken care of.

***

When I got back to Ari's house, Mardi was on her way down the stairs of the stoop. She looked tired and upset. I tried to grab her arm, but she yanked it away from me. "Let me go!"

I frowned. "What the fuck is wrong with you?" I asked, becoming instantly irritated with her. I think I needed a nap or somethin'. It was going on two days since I'd slept.

"Jahmani, why don't you go and ask that bitch in there what's the matter with me? All she been doing since she got back is asking me when you'll return, saying how much she just needed you to hold her. Hold her? You don't even know this bitch! Or do you?" She looked me up and down with her face balled up.

"Yo, you bugging. I met her one time before you brought her over to my pad. She go to my mom's church. I didn't get more than a few sentences in before she shot me down, but that don't matter. Where you finna go?" I reached for her wrist and took ahold of it.

She looked down at it, then up to me. "Why do you care? I thought you and I wasn't together."

My head was pounding. I didn't feel like arguing with her. I could barely keep my eyes open. I wished I had gotten a li'l nap after climbing from between her legs. "Look, Mardi, why don't you just chill here for the night? The streets ain't safe. I ain't gon' be able to sleep unless I know you're good."

"Aw, so you do care?" She crossed her arms in front of her.

The door to Ari's building opened. She stuck her head outside of it. "Jahmani? You're back? Can I talk to you for a minute?" She dabbed at her eyes with the tissue in her left hand and sniffled. Her eyes were puffy. She looked sick.

"Yeah, I'll be right there. Just let me finish this up with Mardi real fast, a'ight?"

She nodded and stepped back into the hallway, closing the door.

Mardi scrunched her face and took a deep breath. "Nigga, I know you ain't just say you were going to finish up with me just so you could run back to that black bitch." She started snapping in Spanish. "You don't even know this bitch! You've been knowing me for all of your life, since we were kids. All of the sudden you're finishing up with me just so you can run back to a bitch you don't know from Adam or Eve? I swear, if I was a nigga, I'd whoop your ass, Jahmani. You're switching up on me, and I think it's only because of this bullshit with Linx. Or maybe it's the Puerto Rico thing. Either way, you are hurting me. Now, I demand you come with me so we can figure some things out. You're hurting me right now. So bad." She stepped past me and stood beside her truck, popping the locks and opening the passenger side. "Come on, *papi*. Let's take a drive."

I didn't feel like doing any of that. I knew if I took a ride with Mardi, we were going to argue for at least an hour. And no matter what conclusion we came too, I knew for a fact I was coming back to check on Ari. I just had to. And because of that, me and Mardi would have gotten into a big fight anyway. I could tell she was jealous, and the worst kind of Puerto Rican woman was a jealous one. I figured I'd nip all of that in the bud, and let her be known what it was right away. "Yo, I ain't fucking wit' you, shorty. I'ma find out what's good wit' her. She just got some real sad news, and somebody should be there to hold her down. Nah mean?"

"And that somebody gotta be you? Are you fucking kidding me?" She slammed her passenger door and walked into my face. "Ooh, you make me so angry. I wanna hit yo' ass right now." She balled her fist and took another step forward.

Now I was angry. I pointed to her truck. "Yo, get yo' ass in the truck and get the fuck out of here. I'ma hit you up on Snapchat later, that's my word. Now, go."

She sucked her teeth. "You know what, Jahmani? Fuck you, nigga. You can have that black bitch. It's good. I knew sooner or later you was gon' cross over, anyway. All you mixed niggas do. I hope you and that bitch live happily ever after. I hate you," she snapped in Spanish before getting in her truck and shooting away from the curb. She slammed on the brakes halfway down the block. "Nigga, I promise you I'll get the last laugh. Trust that. Enjoy that bitch! It's gon' cost you!" Her windows rolled up and she sped back down the street.

I waved her off. "That girl crazy." I shook my head and made it up the stoop's stairs with her threat in the back of my mind. When I stepped into Ari's crib, all of the lights were off. She had candles burning all around. The atmosphere was reminiscent of my mother's place every so often. I had to make it my business to call and check in with her before I laid down. It smelled like she'd lit a few incense. Somali Rose dominated the air. The scent was soothing, to say the least.

"I didn't mean to cause you so much drama. I only told her I wanted to chill with you for a few hours while I got my heart together. I didn't know she was going to go all psycho and whatnot." She was sitting Indian-style on the floor of her front room with her Bible on her lap. Her face was tear-streaked, her nose red. In her left hand was a tissue. She sighed. "Will you sit with me for a minute?" She didn't even look up at me. Her head remained lowered. I could tell she was hurting.

I lowered myself down and sat across from her. "Is there anything I can do to make you feel better? I mean, all you have to do is tell me, and I will." There was a voice in my head that kept on shouting, '*You killed her brother. You watched your cousin kill her cousin. Nigga, you are bogus. Now you sitting across from her hoping she will open her legs to you. You are sick. Go get help!*'

"I know I don't know you like that, but I just really need for you to put your arms around me. I feel so lost right now. I don't know what to do. First my brother, and now my cousin. He was all I had left. Now I'm all alone in this crazy world with nobody to protect me. And it doesn't matter how strong a woman is, she'll always need protection. I need God more than ever."

She lowered her face to her hand and broke down. Her shoulder hopped up and down just a tad. I could hear her sniffling. It broke my heart. While I wasn't regretting killing

132

Mikey and taking part in Mach's death. I felt guilty for the effect it was having on her. I guess niggas like me who killed never really took a time-out to think about how it would affect the family of those they killed. I mean, I never gave a fuck about none of that until this day. I was sick on the stomach, listening to her pain. Man, I wished I could heal her. I don't know why I wished that so bad, but I just did.

I scooted over and slowly placed my arm around her shoulders. She relinquished her power, turned, and laid her face on my chest, really breaking down. Her nails went into my side. "I just don't understand. I prayed for them. I prayed for my brother. I prayed for Mach. Yet God still took them away. Why would He do that?" she cried into me.

Damn, I felt like shit. My eyes got misty. A lump formed in my throat and made it hard for me to swallow. I squeezed my eyelids, and a tear seeped out of the left one and rolled down my face. The snot in my nose loosened, and I had to sniff to keep it from running out. I held her tighter. "Ari, please calm down, goddess. Everything is going to be alright. I promise you."

She shook her head in my chest. "No, it's not. How can you even say that? Mach is dead. Mikey is dead. My parents are dead. There is nobody left but my aunt, and she's so strung out on heroin that she isn't even herself anymore. I'm all alone, Jahmani, and I'm so scared. So scared of what this world has in store for me. I need God so bad right now. I wonder if He's looking down on me with mercy."

"Of course He is. He hasn't allowed for anything to happen to you just yet. That means He has a divine plan for you. You just have to stay the course. Keep your faith."

"If He's looking down on us, then how could He allow for this to happen? I pray to Him every day, ten times a day, asking Him to keep my family safe. Especially Mach because

Mach was all I had left after my brother was murdered in cold blood. But he didn't listen. He didn't listen when I asked Him to keep my parents safe. He didn't listen when I asked him to keep my brother safe. So, what's the use of prayer?" She came out of my arms and stood up, pacing the floor. "What am I going to do? Linx is crazy. Whenever he gets out of that hospital, I know for a fact he is going to come for me. This time he will kill me. You won't be there to protect me, and why should you be after how nasty I was to you in the beginning? I deserve everything that is going to happen to me."

She continued to pace, running her fingers through her hair. I stood up. "Ari, I know you don't know me like that, and there is no reason to trust me, but on my mother, I ain't about to let nothing happen to you. I'll take care of that fool Linx. I know how he get down, so I gotta squash him. It's bigger than you, but it's because of you, as well. You just gotta trust me."

She looked over at me, her shadow cast on the wall behind her. "Why would you want to protect me, though, Jahmani? Why do you look at me the way you do?" She stepped closer to me and looked into my eyes, taking ahold of my hands.

I felt like a simp, so I pulled them away from her. I was a killer at heart, but she had me feeling all soft and stuff. I didn't know how to mentally handle that, so I had to try to keep in touch with the goon side of me. I wanted to tell her I had fallen in love with her at first sight, that ever since I'd laid eyes on her I had not been able to get her off of my mind, but I didn't want to feel soft. Just imagining those words coming out of my mouth made me feel less than a man, so I couldn't utter them. I had to take a more tough-guy approach.

"Yo, you're just super fine to me. I don't know why I'm jocking you so hard. Damn. And as far as Linx go, son ain't have no right putting his mittens on you. Word up. Then he really fucked up by pointing a gun in my face. Kid gotta get what's coming to 'im. I ain't about to let him or no other nigga hurt you. That's my word. Especially after finding out you're out here all alone. That just make me wanna turn up."

I exhaled, and turned my back to her. I didn't know why I was feeling how I was feeling about her. I guess the murders of her brother and cousin had something to do with it. But even more than those, my mother had always told me one day I would find a woman, and she would have such control over my heart that I would not be able to handle it. I didn't know if Ari was that woman or if I even believed what my mother put down to me, but what I did know was I was feeling some type of way about Ari, and I didn't know how to conduct myself around her because of those feelings. I mean, we had no history together. I barely even knew her, yet I felt how I felt. It started to make me angry.

She stepped up to me and placed her hand on my shoulder. "Jahmani, your mother lives in the Bronx River Houses right?"

I turned around to face her. "Yeah, she been staying there for almost ten years now. One day I wanna move her out of those slums. That place ain't fit for a queen. Nah mean?"

She nodded her head. "I do, but that's not the reason I asked you that question. About a month ago they found my brother Mikey murdered in the boiler room downstairs. They haven't been able to piece together what really happened, and they have no leads. But I just figured since your mother stays there and you spend an ample amount of time there, you would have some type of knowledge of who could have killed him? Do you?"

Ghost

Chapter 13

I lowered my head and took a deep breath. I don't know why it was, but that question made me sick on the stomach. I couldn't even look her in the eyes. I wasn't the type of man who liked to lie to anybody, especially not those I respected or cared about. And as crazy as it sounded, I both cared about and respected Ari, but not enough to tell her the truth. I felt like shit.

"Yo, I just heard a few ramblings through the projects, that's all. I guess your brother was a stick-up kid. He'd gotten down on a few cats that could have wanted him dead. Nobody has ever said for sure who did what, so I don't really know what to tell you. I wish I did."

I looked into her eyes and felt like a straight piece of garbage. Damn, my soul wasn't feeling right at all. I was wishing I had never smoked Mikey. I should have just whooped his ass real good and been done with it. Now that I'd met Ari, she had me feeling some type of way. And because I had murdered her brother, I was starting to feel like her and I could never explore transitioning into anything. That crushed me, to say the least.

"Oh, okay. I just thought I might ask because I know you keep your ear to the streets." She touched my right hand and tried to slide hers into it.

Once again I yanked my hand away. Now that I was beginning to see we could never have a future because of the sins I'd committed against her, she was starting to turn me off. I needed to get out of there. It was the only way I could get the unexplainable urges for her out of my system. I needed to leave her presence.

"Look, Shorty, I gotta be on my way. I got a lot of stuff to take care of. I gotta prepare for that nigga Linx, too. I know he gon' be on bullshit whenever he get out of that hospital. I been around him long enough to know how he get down. I hope you feel better, though. Hold ya head up." I brushed past her and made my way to the guest room to grab my shirt I'd taken off earlier that day when I'd fucked Mardi on her kitchen floor.

Ari sped up behind me and grabbed my wrist. "Wait a minute, do you think Linx killed my brother? Or maybe even Mach? I mean, if you think he'd come at you and you're his cousin, then he had to've, right?"

I stood there for a minute, looking into her beautiful face. I was once again mesmerized by her butter pecan complexion, the almond-shaped eyes, the deep dimples, and the scent of her. Her hair fell along her shoulder. She was so sexy to me. I had to shake my head in order to snap out of the zone she had me placed in. I had to bring that street shit back to the forefront.

I yanked my hand away from her. "Yo, fuck you think, I'm a snitch or something, shorty? Huh? You think you can smile in my face and some type of pussy'll come out of me? That it, huh?"

She shook her head. "No, it's nothing like that at all. I'm just hurting, Jahmani. I need to know what happened and who did what so I can have closure in my heart. There is no closure there for either one of them, and because there isn't, there is no peace within me. I know I'm grasping at straws, but please try and understand. I am begging you." Tears slowly blinked out of her eyes.

I was close to caving in. I hated to see her cry. I wanted to snatch her up and hold her close within my embrace. I knew fifty percent of her pain was caused by me. The other fifty percent I had assisted in, as well. I felt like a dog of a man. I didn't understand how the remorse over their murders was eating at me so bad. I was sure my heart was as cold as ice, but then I had to meet her. Why did I ever have to meet Ari?

"Yo, I ain't no snitch, and I don't know what happened to either one of those dudes. Maybe you'll find out one day, but clearly coming at me ain't gon' get you nowhere." I bumped her, went into the guest room, and grabbed my shirt with a frown on my face. When I stepped back into the short hallway, she was standing there with her hand on the wall, blocking my path. The hallway was narrow enough to do so.

"Yo, watch out, shorty. I gotta get out of here. Word up." I moved her arm and nudged her out of the way.

"Wait! Please, Jahmani." She rushed back in front of me and blocked my path, her face wet with tears. I refused to look in her face. It was making me too weak, so I looked everywhere but there.

"Get out of my way, Ari. Damn. I gotta get the fuck out of here. Being here is driving me nuts."

"Look, I know I don't know you, and I know you don't care about me or nothing like that, but I just gotta be honest with you. I'm scared of what Linx is going to do to me. Deep in my heart, I really think he is the one who killed Mikey. I don't know why I feel that way, but it is very strong on my spirit. Mach is dead now. Mikey and Mach were the only two protectors I had left on this earth. Now I am all alone, and I'm scared. Can you please just stay with me for a few days? At least until I can get myself back and make some sort of arrangements? I'll even pay you for each day if I have to. Wait here, I got about a hundred bucks tucked away. She rushed down the hall toward her bedroom, opening the door, then paused, looking over her shoulder at me. "You aren't going to leave, are you?"

I walked toward her. "Wait a minute. Less than an hour ago you wasn't giving me no play. You even acting a little standoffish. Now you're saying you don't want me to leave? That you feel secure with me protecting you?" I shook my head. "Nall, shorty, fuck that. I don't trust you. I feel like you're up to something. Don't nobody flip that quick. I'm out of here."

I turned my back on her and made my way to the front door, opened it, and stepped into the hallway. She rushed and caught me before I closed it. She flipped the light on in her front room, looking over her shoulder back into the house as if she was waiting for somebody to jump out at her.

"All of this dang ol' killing and murders is not normal. I've lost two people that were close to me in less than a month. Why don't I have the right to be scared? I'm alone, Jahmani." She continued to look out at me, then back into her apartment.

Damn, I was feeling so bogus. I knew I needed to be there to hold her down. After all, she had a valid point. She was just a female, and both Mikey and Mach had been killed quite heinously. It was enough for anybody to be spooked out of their mind. The more I looked into her face, the weaker I got. I just could not leave her out on a limb like that.

I exhaled and lowered my head again. "Damn, Ari, what do you want me to do?" I asked, stepping back into her apartment.

***

We sat on the carpet of her living room with the television on, but no sound. She sat Indian-style across from me. In the middle of us were playing cards. We were playing a game called King's Corner. She'd just taught it to me, and already I was whooping her butt in it. One thing I noticed right away was she hated to lose. Little frown lines would appear across her forehead when she lost a hand, but when she won her dimples would be popping. I was so smitten by the complexion of her skin, the thickness of her hair, and of course that natural scent of her. Though I'd never sat down to play a card game, I was having the time of my life.

She laid a three of hearts on top of a two of spades and smiled. There was one card left in her hand. I knew she thought for sure she would be winning the hand soon, but I had other plans in mind.

She looked over at me with a curious look on her face. "Can I ask you a question, Jahmani? And I need for you to be really honest with me. Oh, and it's your go."

I laid a ten of hearts on top of a jack of spades after pulling a card and nodded my head. I had three cards left in my hand, and I was nervous about losing this hand. I was a sore loser. I didn't care who I was losing to. I mean, I enjoyed the view of her thick thighs that were on display because of the tight purple shorts she was wearing and the hint of belly I could see under her half t-shirt. She had a diamond in her navel, and it looked so good there. Her stomach was a caramel color, but the closer it got to the navel region, the darker her skin became. It was so sexy to me. Man, I couldn't stop stealing glances at her.

"You can ask me anything as long as it don't have anything to do with Mach or Mikey. Not Linx, either. I'm trying to get them three out of my mind for a minute. Go 'head."

She grabbed a card from the deck and put it into her hand. She looked down at the other cards with her left eyebrow raised. "Why are black females the lowest on the totem pole when it comes to men choosing?"

That caught me off guard. I sat up and looked across at her. "What do you mean?" I asked, now paying as close attention as I could. I was expecting her to go a whole different route.

"What I've noticed, even in Baltimore, is whenever the dudes in the hood came up on a lot of cash, or whenever they wanted to stunt on other dudes, they would do it by going to get either a Spanish female or even a white girl. Every now and then I'd see an Asian here and there, but for the most part it was either white or Spanish. Then they'd go for the ones who have bodies that are shaped like us sistas. Whether their shapes are real or fake, they didn't care. And it's like we're good enough for them to put a baby in us, but when they think long-term it's always with a different race. Why is that?"

I situated myself on the carpet and wiped a trace of sweat from my forehead. Damn, I was caught off guard. "Uh, yo, I don't know why that is. I think most niggas just like what's different. We grow up seeing black women all the time, so that's normal. But when we look outside of our women, we see all of this natural long hair, light skin, different languages and scents, and it makes us feel like we're missing out on something. Then most cats look to the whole mating process of it all. We want real cute kids, and the one way to avoid getting an average-looking child is to mate with a woman of a different race. That way we can get the curly hair and pretty eyes, which are important to most men when it comes to their daughters. Don't no man want an ugly-ass daughter or son. I know I don't."

She laid out all of her cards, winning the hand. "So, you think if you mated with a full-bred black woman and y'all had kids, those kids with her would be ugly because they aren't all mixed-up, gene-wise?" She looked into my eyes, challenging.

"I'm not necessarily saying that, but you gotta admit mixed kids are cuter than full-blown black shorties." I was getting more and more hot. I felt like I had two sweaters on and a jacket when, in actuality, I was sitting there in my wife-beater. I grabbed the cards and started to shuffle them.

"Well, I think our race of women are the most beautiful. I love who I am, and I don't need to be mixed up in order to sit at the top of the totem pole. My whole life I've heard my brother and cousin go on and on about Spanish girl this, white girl that, Indian chick this, and Asian girl that. They spoke about their beauty and everything in between. They used words and phrased to describe them as if they were the rarest and most sacred women ever created. Then, when it came to them describing our women, they used nothing but derogatory language. It was this 'B' this, or that 'H' that, and it only got worse from there. So much so that for the longest of time growing up as a little girl, I always saw myself as lower than Latinos, whites, and any other race that was lighter than me. I never even saw myself as beautiful until I was approached by a recruiter from the modeling agency four months ago."

I couldn't believe what I was hearing because, to me, Ari was one of the finest women I had ever seen in my entire life. I'd messed with nothing but Spanish women, and in my opinion none of them were on her level. Not even Mardi.

I started to deal the cards. "Ari, I swear, you are probably the most beautiful woman I have ever seen in my life. I mean, the first day I saw you in church, I just had to say something."

She shook her head. "Thank you for the compliment. It is flattering. But let me ask you this question: how many black women have you actually dated? I mean, especially living in the Bronx where everywhere you look there is a different race of female. How many times have you overlooked a female of my race because you found another one more attractive from another?"

I pulled my collar away from my neck. I wanted to lie to her so bad because I didn't know where she was going with things, but I just couldn't. I had to keep it real with her. "I ain't never been with a full-blooded sista before. In fact, I've only dated Latin women. I always thought they were the most sexy all around the board, until I met you." I blushed after saying the last part, and I didn't know why. I ain't never been the type to feel so taken aback by a woman, but there was just something about Ari. She made me weak at the wrong times. She made me question my own thoughts and feelings. I was confused.

She looked over at me and turned her head slightly to the side. "Thank you for being honest with me. I was sure you were going to go the other way with that." She picked up her cards and put them in order. "So, you really think I'm beautiful?"

I nodded. "Yeah, you really are. I ain't got no reason to gas you up. I can tell the gas prices are too high when it comes to you. You're not one of those average women. You tend to look deeper than the surface, which is what's really good. I like you, though. I gotta admit that." I smiled at her. "Go first, because I dealt."

I couldn't look into her eyes because I was feeling some type of way. I'd never been one of them mushy-type of niggas. This was the first time for me, and I felt weird. I couldn't see myself getting used to feeling like I was feeling.

She pulled a card, and then laid more cards down on the carpet until she was left holding only two of the eight she started with. "So, aren't you going to ask me how many black boys I've dated, and how many from the other races?"

That thought never even crossed my mind because I didn't want to imagine her with anybody else. In my own head I wanted to think that whenever we crossed that threshold, I would be her first for every thing. I was jealous, and me and her weren't even together. "Yeah, go ahead and tell me."

"I've dated three black boys in my life, the rest have all been Latino. Why? Because it was instilled within me by the men around me that every other race was more beautiful than my own. So, when I looked for beauty, I looked for the opposite of my reflection in the mirror. The three black boys I dated were when I was in the first grade. They lasted no more than two days apiece," she laughed. "But I just wanted to let you know that so you didn't think I was judging you. I'm no better than you are."

She ran her fingers through her hair and moved her thighs slightly. The shorts went further into her gap, molding to her sex lips. I had visions of sticking my nose right in her center and sniffing her up.

"What made you ask me that question about black women and the whole totem pole thing, anyway?" I was curious, and my piece was standing tall in my jeans. I needed to find a way to adjust him, because it hurt. I needed to stop looking between her legs, too. It was driving me more and more crazy.

She shrugged her shoulders. "It was just a question I've always wanted to ask my brother or Mach, but I'll never get that chance." She sighed. "I'm sorry, I know you said to not bring them up. I'm trying. I really am."

I played a few cards and went out on her. "That's game." I stood up and stretched my legs, yawning with my arms reaching way over my head, forgetting the fact I was as hard as a gangbanger. My eyes got bucked, and I tried to block it with my hands. Looking down, I caught her looking up at me. "That's my bad, Ari. You just got me feeling some type of way."

She stood up and pulled her little shorts out of her crease. "It's good. You're only human. Are you hungry?" She walked past me and made her way into the kitchen. Her shorts were all in her booty, exposing the bottom halves of her brown cheeks. They were darker than the rest of her skin. With each step she took, they jiggled. It was making me harder and harder. I had to reach into my pants and pull my log upward so it laid along my stomach. I pulled the beater over it to cover the head that was outside of my waistband, throbbing.

"Yeah, what you got in here?" I followed her into the kitchen keeping my eyes planted on that juicy backside. I wondering what she tasted like on my tongue. I imagined my tongue sawing in and out of her rose bud while my chin tickled her clit.

She opened the refrigerator and popped back on her legs. "Let's see here. I can heat up what we ate earlier, or I got some leftover lasagna in here. If that don't tickle your fancy, we can eat a few bowls of cereal. What do you want to do?"

What I had on my mind I knew wasn't appropriate. "Yo, to be honest, I gotta get a move on. I need to check on my moms and my brother's kid. I enjoyed spending time with you, though."

She closed the refrigerator and started to bite on her nail. "Uh, well, can you just do me one last favor, and then you can go?" she asked, stepping into my face and looking up at me with those pretty brown eyes of hers.

I looked into them and got weaker. I didn't know what the fuck was going on, man. Damn, I needed to get out of her house, fast. "Yeah, what favor is that?"

"Can you please just hold me until I fall asleep? I'm so tired, but I know once you leave I'm going to be up and so paranoid I won't be able to rest. I would really appreciate it."

I needed any reason to get behind her, so holding her was right up my alley. There was no way I could have turned her down.

Ten minutes later, and after a bowl of Cookie Crisp cereal, we climbed into her queen size bed. She pulled the blanket back, along with a sheet, and got in, holding it open for me to do the same thing. "Come on, Jahmani. Don't be scared."

Scared I was not. Nervous? That was a different story. I didn't know if I could be so close to her without going too far. I had never been so infatuated by any woman in my entire life.

I dropped my jeans and climbed into the bed with her. She lay on her side, and I scooted right behind her until the back of her head was right against my chest. She smelled so good this close up. Her warmth radiated back to me. Her rounded backside was right in my lap. It felt soft and inviting. I scooted forward to feel it better, my pipe telescoping all on its own.

She moaned and arched her back. "Maybe you shouldn't be so close, Jahmani. I can feel you throbbing down there." Her voice was strained. Her teeth bit into her juicy bottom lip.

"Yo, it's good. I know how to behave myself. Just relax ma." I scooted closer and held her waist. I could feel a stretch mark along it. It sent a shiver through me.

"Okay, well, I'ma trust you. Hold me tighter, and promise me you'll protect me. I'm so scared. Life is so short."

I closed my eyes and shook my head behind her. Damn, I didn't know what was wrong with me. Every time she said she was scared, I felt like killing something. I wouldn't never let nobody hurt her if I could prevent it. The tighter I held her, the more I hated Linx, and I knew I had to kill him so he would never get the chance to hurt her.

"I got you, Ari."

Instead of me holding her for just that night, I wound up staying with her for the next three days, getting to know the real her and giving her pieces of me I didn't even know existed. And every night we'd wind back up in the same position with me holding her until we both fell asleep.

Ghost

Chapter 14

It was the fourth day after me and Linx had gotten into it. Ari woke me up by shaking my shoulder. "Jahmani. Jahmani. Wake up. Mardi is on the phone, and she's talking crazy. I think you need to get an understanding with her." She dropped the phone on my chest and stood by the entranceway to her room with her arms crossed in front of her. She looked angry. A toothbrush was in her left hand with a blue gel on it.

I sat all the way up so my back was against the headboard. I yawned into my fist, and my eyes became watery. "Yo, what's good, Mardi? Why you calling shorty's phone talking all crazy and shit?"

She scoffed. "Damn, this bitch got you fighting her battles now? Well, ain't that somethin'?" she laughed. "Nigga, you musta been so far in her pussy that you ain't figured out I got yo' trifling-ass." She sucked her teeth and was quiet.

I yawned again and shook my head. I didn't know why I was so tired. Me and Ari had gone to sleep at, like, ten o'clock. Because I'd just woken up, my dick was sticking up in my boxers, jumping up and down. I squeezed it with my right hand to calm it. "Yo, what the fuck you talking about, shorty?"

"Five hundred thousand dollars, nigga. That's what I'm talking about. You wanna shit on me for that bitch? Well, I'm finna spend every penny of this money like I'm Blue Cantrell. Fuck you, Jahmani. I hope you and that bitch rot in hell. That nigga Linx gon' fuck you over like you did me when he catch you."

The phone went dead. I sat there looking at it for a long time. It took a while for everything she'd said to register in my head.

"Jahmani, you know I don't like when you call me shorty. Is it too much to ask for you to use my name?" Ari asked, walking toward the bed. She had on some tight, pink Victoria's Secret booty shorts and a pink halter that showed off the top swells of her breasts. She looked like Heaven, and good enough to eat.

I jumped out of the bed and bumped her accidentally while running out of the room. Everything Mardi had said hit me all at once. I knew this bitch couldn't have been grimy enough to hit me for my stash.

I rushed into the guest room and grabbed the book bag from under the bed. I nearly broke my fingers trying to unzip it. I was already starting to panic because it felt so light. When I opened it all the way. I fell to my knees. It was empty. "Aw, fucking Mardi!"

I picked up my phone and dialed her number over and over. Each time she ignored the call. Finally, I sat on the edge of the bed and texted her, telling her to pick up the damn phone. Then I tried to call her again.

My phone vibrated. All happy-faced emojis from her. Then the number "$500,000" came across the screen.

Ari stepped into the doorway. "Are you okay, Jahmani? You look like you're about to throw up. Are you hungry?"

Once again I rushed past her and back into her bedroom. Slipping my feet into my Jordans, I grabbed my pistol from under her bed and felt my heart pounding in my chest. Then I was back in the hallway with a mug on my face.

"Jahmani, can you talk to me? What is going on?" Ari asked, looking worried. "Are you regretting staying here with me?"

I shook my head as I jogged to her front door. "Look, I'll holler at you later. Keep this door locked. I'll text you before I come. You hear me?" I shouted toward her.

"I hear you! But what did she say? Why are you leaving?" she asked, walking toward the door. Her voice was breaking up.

I closed the door and jogged down the stairs, rushing out of her building into a rainstorm. Lightning flashed across the sky. Rain pelted the sidewalk violently. The scent of it was all in the air. No more than five feet out of the building, I found myself drenched. I rushed to my car and pulled open the door, got in, and smashed away from the curb. The tires spun for a brief second before enough traction was established for me to pull off. I tried Mardi's number again. Still no answer.

"I know this bitch ain't do this. I know this bitch ain't stuck me for my paper!" I yelled, slamming my hands on the steering wheel. My clothes were matted to me, and I felt itchy. "Man, on my mother, if this bitch hit my stash, I'ma kill her ass. Fuck our history! Word is bond!"

I made a crazy left, and my car fish-tailed before straightening out. I stepped on the gas again and sped until I got in front of my building. Once there, I threw the car in park and hopped out. I rushed up the stairs of my stoop and into the hallway. I stayed on the third floor. I slipped four times before I made it to my door, then dropped my keys twice before I could get the house key into the lock. I turned it and pushed my way into my crib, falling to my knees from the sheer force of my hysteria.

Jumping up, I rushed into the back of the apartment, right where the hallway ended. As soon as I got there, I almost threw up all over the floor because the first thing I saw was the grill of my vent lying right on the floor beside it. There was a little piece of garbage bag attached to it.

Still in disbelief, I got on my knees, stuck my head into the vent, and looked down it. It was empty. I threw up in my mouth and scooted backward until I was on my haunches. "This dirty bitch done fucked me like this! Aw, hell nall!"

I called her number a thousand times until finally she

picked up, laughing at the top of her lungs. "Mardi, on everything I love, bring me my muthafucking money. Stop playing wit' me!" I snapped, feeling like I was about to pass out because I was so vexed. I'd never been this mad before.

She laughed louder. "Nigga, I told you I was gon' get the last laugh. Didn't I say that? Well ha-muthafuckin'-ha. You wanna shit on me for that black bitch? Hold a bunch of bullshit over my head? Well, nigga, I'ma leave wit' a bang. I hate you, Jahmani. You hurt me. You hurt me worse than any man ever has. You know I loved your half-breed ass, and you shitted on me. Shitted on me for a black bitch that ain't even in my league. Damn, you niggas are trifling. You'll never find me. I'ma put this money to good use. Oh, and I told Linx where that bitch stay. I hope he fuck her up and then take a good look at you. Have a nice life, you rotten son of a bitch. I hope that nigga make you happier than I ever did. She sho gon' cost you a lot."

The phone went dead. I dropped it to the carpet. It bounced once and wound up on its face. I fell to my knees and buried my forehead on the carpet. I felt so stupid. Mardi had been the only person I'd ever shown my stash spot. The only person I trusted to know where it was besides my mother. I just knew she would never cross me for it. But I had been wrong.

I was so sick that I jumped up and ran to the bathroom, lifted the lid of the toilet, and purged my guts. Not only was that five hundred thousand dollars in cash, but it was blood money. I would have to go at my cousin to the death over it. I had plans on using a nice portion of it to buy my mother a house out in Queens. Now it was gone, and I was back to square one. I dry-heaved and threw up some more. I didn't have much food in my stomach, mostly cereal, and I had only eaten a bowl of that.

After I was sure I couldn't purge anymore, I sat on the

floor and grabbed a roll of tissue, taking a small amount to wipe my mouth before throwing it inside the toilet and flushing it. I sat there for five minutes trying to get my head together. I kept seeing visions of Mardi laughing at the top of her lungs while she pranced through the mall, buying up a bunch of stuff, pointing at random items while the sales girls broke their necks to grab them for her.

I covered my face with my hands and jumped up. I couldn't accept this. I couldn't let this bitch do me in like this. I refused.

I rushed into my bedroom and pulled out my top drawer, grabbed a .40 Glock, and slammed a clip into the bottom of it. I put it on my waist, then grabbed its twin with nothing but murder on my mind. If Mardi thought I was soft enough to play with, then I was about to turn up the heat on her ass. *It's always fun and games until somebody gets hurt,* I thought as I grabbed my car keys and rushed out of my building.

***

I slammed on my brakes in front of Mardi's father's small home, threw my car in park, and jumped out of it. I rushed up the steps to his place with the rain coming down so hard I could barely see in front of me. The wind threatened to knock me over. New York City was feeling the effects of Tropical Storm Florence, which had crashed into the Carolinas, causing major destruction.

Ding-dong! Ding-dong! Ding-dong! I pressed the doorbell over and over. He had a porch light, and it looked like a million mosquitoes were flying all around it. They were all in my face and everything. This only got me more annoyed, especially when I felt one bite me on the cheek. I smacked it on my face and saw there were traces of blood on my hand. "Muthafucka bit me," I said aloud, angry. I wiped the dead bug on the house, along with the blood. I rang the doorbell over and over, getting more and more furious by the second.

"Hold on. Hold on. Hold. Lord, have mercy. I'm coming," I heard Mason say. I knew his voice anywhere. He was Mardi's father, and me and the man had never gotten along. For as long as I had been a part of Mardi's life, he'd always tried to break us apart or give her a hard time for being with me. He was full-blooded Puerto Rican, but he acted more white. He seemed to dislike his race of people, and any other that wasn't white. He was 5'10" tall and heavyset with a big nose and green eyes. His breath always stunk to me.

He pulled back the curtain, and seconds later he opened the door to his small home. "Boy, what are you doing beating on my door like you've lost the best part of your mind? Why, I have a mind to step out of this house and kick your ass. What do you want?" he snapped with his face screwed up. His breath smelled like cabbage and shit. He had the nerve to be chewing gum, but it had to have long lost its flavor and scent.

"Yo, where is Mardi? I need to talk to her now." I tried my best to keep my composure. I could feel my blood already boiling.

The wind picked up, and my clothes wagged like a flag. My face was drenched with rain, and on top of that the place where I'd been bitten by the mosquito was starting to itch like crazy. I tried to pay it no mind, but it was so hard. I scratched it and looked up to him, on the verge of losing my cool.

He bucked his eyes. "I know you ain't brought yo' monkey-ass over here looking for my daughter. And you know I don't like you or nothing you stand for. You gots to be out of your freaking mind if you think I'ma tell you anything." He leaned further out of the house as if to invade my space on purpose.

154

Lightning flashed behind me before thunder roared so loud it sounded like it was right next to my ear. I shivered and lowered my head. "Mason, your daughter took something from me. All I need to know if she was over here today. You can keep all that other slick shit to yourself. Answer my question."

He pointed. "Get the fuck off my porch, and don't worry about whether my child been here or not. It is none of your concern. You got five seconds to get back in your car and drive —"

I turned, grabbed him by the neck with my left hand, and stuck the pistol in his face with my right. I forced him into the hallway of his house and cocked the hammer. He fell on his back in the hallway with me right on top of him, the gun pressed into his right eye socket. "Listen here, you tough-ass old man. Tell me where the fuck your daughter is or I'ma leave your brains all over this welcome mat. I ain't playing, neither. Where the fuck is she?" I growled into his fat face.

He stared into my eyes and frowned. "I don't know where she is. She came through here a few hours ago and gave me a bunch of money and a Rolex watch, the one she told me she was gon' get me for my 55th birthday. After she gave it to me, she hugged me and left. That's all I can tell you. Why? What have you gotten her into, Jahmani? You ain't nothing but a damn thug," he spat with sweat all over his forehead.

"Where is your phone, old man?" I asked, grabbed him by the collar and trying to pull his big-ass into the house some more. He twisted away from me and beat at my hand until it was free.

"Take your filthy hands off of me, you brute. I'm not afraid of you. Get the fuck out of my house! Now!" he ordered.

"What?" *Bam. Bam. Bam. Bam. Bam. Bam.* I smacked him across the face with the Glock over and over. All of my pent-up frustration coupled with the utter disdain I'd carried for him throughout the years. It all came to the forefront. By the time I got ahold of myself, he lay on the floor in front of me in a bloody mess, his face swelled up like gigantic brown raspberry. I was out of breath. I stood up, looking down on him. "Where is your fucking phone, Mason? I ain't got time for this shit!"

He sat up and spit blood into his lap. I watched his right eye close up and turn black. Blood dripped out of his mouth and ran down his neck, saturating his button-up shirt. He pointed toward the kitchen. "It's on the table. You ain't have to do me like this, Jahmani. You're an animal," he spat and fell onto his elbow.

I rushed into the kitchen and grabbed his phone, then walked
back in and gave it to him. "Call Mardi and ask her where she is. Hurry up!" I pointed the gun in his face. His blood was streaked all over it. The sight only excited the goon in me.

He took the phone and dialed Mardi's number, placing the phone to his ear. He closed his eyes and swallowed a mouthful of blood. "Hello, princess. Where are you?" he asked. He opened his eyes wide and closed them again. His right hand shook. Blood dripped off of his bottom lip. "Because I need to know. I am worried about you. Where are you?"

I snatched the phone from him. "Bitch, if you don't give me back my shit, I'm finna smoke yo' old man. I know he all you got left, so it's in yo' best interest to give me back my money!"

"What are you doing at my father's house, Jahmani? This ain't got nothing to do with him," she hollered into the phone.

I held his phone out and took a picture of him, then sent it to her. "You see that shit? This nigga one bullet away from death. Give me back my money or shit about to get real bloody for you. Word to my mother. I'm tired of– Aw!" I felt a sharp pain in my thigh. I looked down and saw Mason had taken a switch blade and slammed it into me before twisting it, bringing me to one knee.

"You motherfucker! You ain't nothing but the devil!" He pulled it out of my thigh and brought it full-speed toward my throat.

Ghost

Chapter 15

I saw the blade coming at me full-speed. Its destination was my throat. I blocked its path with my gun at the last moment. The blade slamming into the side of my right hand, cutting me open. "Fuck!"

I dropped the gun and kicked Mason in the chest so hard I fell on my back. I could hear him gasping for air. He wheezed as if he had asthma or something. I gathered myself quickly and spotted my gun under his kitchen table where the phone had been. My eyes got big as I made my way toward it, my wrist dripping my fluids.

Mason came to his knees, then dove under the table. He took ahold of the gun, aimed at me, and fired five quick rounds. *Boom. Boom. Boom. Boom. Boom.* The bullets slammed into the wall and the refrigerator behind me, leaving big holes in the drywall. I could hear the *pew!* sound of the bullets as they whizzed past me.

"You motherfucker! Die, you son of a bitch!" he hollered. *Boom. Boom. Boom. Boom. Boom. Boom.*

I fell to my stomach and low-crawled out of the kitchen just as one of the bullets hit me in the right ass cheek and left thigh. It felt like I was on fire, the pain so intense I hollered at the top of my lungs, rolled, and wound up in the hallway with blood running down to my ankle and into my sock. I clenched my teeth together. Tears ran down my face from the pain. I was in agony.

I took the other Glock off my hip and placed my back against the wall. I could hear what sounded like the table crashing to the floor, then his shoes squeaking against the linoleum. My heart pounded in my chest.

"Where are you, you son of a bitch? How dare you come into my house and do this to me? I'ma kill ya! I'ma kill ya if it's the last thing I do," he promised.

I placed my hand over the back of my thigh where the blood was spilling out. It oozed over my fingers. The other bullet had to be lodged in my ass cheek, and it felt like a million needles digging into me. Needles that were on fire. My leg began to shake uncontrollably, threatening to buckle. I swallowed my spit and took a deep breath. This old man was going to kill me. I knew that for a fact.

I heard the sound of his footsteps getting closer. His shadow appeared on the wall of the hallway. Sweat slid down my back. My shoe was soaked with my blood. I slowly lowered myself to both knees, aimed my gun, and waiting for him to come into the hallway.

I had to kill him and find his daughter, get my money back, then get these bullets out of me. Fuck, how could Mardi do this to me? This was a complete blindside if I had ever witnessed one.

"You're dead, Jahmani. Dead. I should have killed you a long time ago!" he hollered and rushed into the hallway in a frenzy.

I lowered my eyes and smiled through the pain at the same time. Then I was finger-fucking my Glock and watching him fill with hole after hole. He dropped the gun after the third bullet ripped into his chin, his eyes wide open. He fell to his knees, and I was still lighting him up. The gun jumping in my hand, smoke rising from it and wafting to the ceiling. When his face hit the floor, a big puddle formed around him. I jumped up, rushed over, and grabbed my gun from him. "Bitch-ass old man. You made this happen. I was just gon' fuck you up a li'l bit, but now look at you. Damn."

When I grabbed his phone off the floor, Mardi was on it in a panic. "Daddy? Daddy? Did you get him? Did you get him, Daddy? Please tell me you got him," she cried.

Instead of saying anything, I simply hung up the phone and fell against the table. My leg had gone out on me. I stayed leaning against it for ten minutes, then got up and cleaned up our mess as best I could before throwing his big-ass into my truck, wrapped in blankets. Then I wrapped my leg and went back in to finish my cleaning. I wiped off everything I felt I touched, grabbed his phone, and bounced from there.

I covered my driver's seat with black garbage bags before I got back behind the wheel and pulled away from the curb. It was raining so bad that even with my windshield wipers on high, I could barely see. There was barely any traction on the streets. Lightning flashed across the sky every few seconds. I watched a tree get struck and fall into the road. I slammed on my brakes about thirty feet from it, and my car slid all the way up to it and bumped it. "Fuck!"

I backed the car down the street just as my phone vibrated in the passenger seat. I grabbed it and placed it to my ear. "What's good?"

A sharp pain shot up my right leg. I winced and clenched my teeth. I had to get to Ari. She had to get these bullets out of me. Going to a hospital was too risky. I couldn't stand any police contact right now. They would for sure put me in jail for 72 hours until they found out what was going on. By that time I imagined Mardi going to them and claiming I'd done something to her father. I assumed she'd recorded the events. I couldn't put anything past her.

"Jahmani. Jahmani. You gotta come and get me. They talking about killing me. Please come and get me," Samantha screamed into the phone. She sounded hysterical and out of breath.

I turned the car all the way around and headed in the opposite direction. The front windshield was being splattered with rain. The streets were so flooded I worried I would get trapped if I didn't get off of them soon. Tropical Storm Florence was kicking the city's ass in a major way. Lightning flashed across the sky, and then the entire street went black. So did the one next to it, and as far down as I could see. I started to panic just a bit.

"Yo, who the fuck are you talking about, ma?" The last thing I needed was to get wrapped up in Samantha's bullshit right now. I had two bullets in me and Mardi's father dead in the trunk of my car. I had to get rid of him and get these bullets out of me.

"Beans! Beans, the head of the Dyse Avenue Crips. He knows Chase is dead, and he'd demanding his money. He thinks I had something to do with him being murdered. They are threatening to kill my daughter. Please come and get me so I can give this money back. I can't do it on my own. They will kill me for sure," she shouted into the phone, causing my ear to ring. I hated when people did that.

"Yo, stop all that fucking hollering, Samantha. That ain't gon' get us nowhere, word up. Where are you right now?" I asked, driving through a puddle of water that made the car float for a little while. Luckily I was able to find traction again, but the streets were getting horrible. I could smell Mason's flesh and blood radiating from the trunk. The scent of death was potent.

"I'm three blocks away from the projects, over on East 171st. I'm sitting in Checkers. Come and get me, please."

That was on my way anyway. I needed to get to my mother's crib so I could make sure she was straight. Now that Samantha was saying them Crip niggas was talking about fucking with Lonnie, that took things to a whole other level. I worried not only for her safety, but my mother's. Even though there were eighteen floors to her building, everybody knew everybody. Them Crip niggas had to know my mother was

Lonnie's grandmother. At least, that's how I felt. So I needed to get over there and get them out of that project building, like, ASAP.

I had a mind to kick Samantha's ass for not thinking things through thoroughly before she made moves, but my brother hadn't taught her anything about the game. I felt like she was just putting the pieces of the puzzle together as she went along.

When I pulled up in front of Checkers, the sign was short circuiting before it went completely out. There was a flash of lightning across the sky, and then a big boom. All of the stoplights went out. Two cars slammed into each other. There was the distinct sound of crunching metal. I turned to see the aftermath of a head-on collision.

Samantha climbed into the passenger's seat and slammed the door. "I gotta get this money over to them or they're going to kill Lonnie. I know they will. Beans ain't somebody to play with," she whimpered. She covered her face with her hands and broke into a fit of sobs. "Please, don't let them hurt my baby."

I pulled out of the parking lot in ten times more pain than I had been in when I arrived. I felt woozy. I could tell I was losing a nice amount of blood. "Yo, shorty, shut the fuck up with that panicking shit. Lonnie gon' be good. That nigga just probably want his scratch. Just make up a story he'll buy. Long as he got his bread, he shouldn't give a fuck about Chase's rapist-ass. Nah mean?" I pulled onto the street and passed the car accident. It looked bad, but it appeared both parties were okay, which was a blessing within itself.

"Let's just hurry and get to Lonnie, Jahmani. Beans wants me to drop this money off to him on the fifth floor. I was supposed to do it thirty minutes ago, but I had to wait for you. I wasn't about to face them by myself. I got a feeling they'd kill me with no remorse." Tears ran down her face. "I gotta get right. I'm so worried." She pulled out an envelope full of white powder, took a pinky nail full, and tooted it up her nostrils. First one, and then the other. She closed it and put it back into her purse, closing her eyes and sitting back. "Life is a bitch."

I shook my head and tried not to pay attention to the scent of Mason or the intense pain I was in.

***

I struggled to make it up the last flight of stairs of my mother's project building. My entire right side felt numb. My Jordan on my right foot was full of blood, so much so that every time I took a step, it spilled over the top of the shoe. I took a deep breath and kept on going.

I got to the doorway of the staircase when my phone buzzed. I looked at the face and saw Ari's picture. Below it, a text:

Jahmani, he's here! Help me! Help me, please!

I froze in place as Samantha shot past me and into the hallway that led to my mother's apartment. I called Ari's number back and limped in pursuit of Samantha. Every step hurt worse than the one before it, yet I kept pressing on.

I watched Samantha turn the corner. My mother's apartment was three doors over from the corner. I limped and limped with the phone to my ear. It rang and rang, then clicked off. I stopped and dialed Ari's number again, worried out of my mind. Who could she have been talking about? Was it Linx? It had to be, right?

I turned the corner just as Samantha froze in her tracks. She placed both hands to her face and screamed, "Oh my God! No. Please, God, no!" She pushed the door open to my mother's apartment and fell to her knees.

I limped faster, and made it to her side, just as Ari came

on to the phone.

"Jahmani! Jahmani! Please, help me!"

To Be Continued...
A Bronx Tale 2
Coming Soon

Submission Guideline

Submit the first three chapters of your completed manuscript to ldpsubmissions@gmail.com, subject line: Your book's title. The manuscript must be in a .doc file and sent as an attachment. Document should be in Times New Roman, double spaced and in size 12 font. Also, provide your synopsis and full contact information. If sending multiple submissions, they must each be in a separate email.

Have a story but no way to send it electronically? You can still submit to LDP/Ca$h Presents. Send in the first three chapters, written or typed, of your completed manuscript to:

LDP: Submissions Dept
Po Box 870494
Mesquite, Tx 75187

DO NOT send original manuscript. Must be a duplicate.

Provide your synopsis and a cover letter containing your full contact information.

Thanks for considering LDP and Ca$h Presents.

A Bronx Tale

Coming Soon from Lock Down Publications/Ca$h Presents

BOW DOWN TO MY GANGSTA

By **Ca$h**

TORN BETWEEN TWO

By **Coffee**

BLOOD STAINS OF A SHOTTA **III**

By **Jamaica**

STEADY MOBBIN **III**

By **Marcellus Allen**

BLOOD OF A BOSS **V**

By **Askari**

LOYAL TO THE GAME **IV**

LIFE OF SIN

By **T.J. & Jelissa**

A DOPEBOY'S PRAYER **II**

By **Eddie "Wolf" Lee**

IF LOVING YOU IS WRONG... **III**

LOVE ME EVEN WHEN IT HURTS **II**

By **Jelissa**

TRUE SAVAGE **VI**

By **Chris Green**

BLAST FOR ME **III**

A BRONX TALE **II**

By **Ghost**

ADDICTIED TO THE DRAMA **III**

By **Jamila Mathis**

Ghost

LIPSTICK KILLAH **III**

CRIME OF PASSION **II**

By **Mimi**

WHAT BAD BITCHES DO **III**

KILL ZONE **II**

By **Aryanna**

THE COST OF LOYALTY **II**

By **Kweli**

SHE FELL IN LOVE WITH A REAL ONE **II**

By **Tamara Butler**

LOVE SHOULDN'T HURT **III**

RENEGADE BOYS **II**

By **Meesha**

CORRUPTED BY A GANGSTA **III**

By **Destiny Skai**

A GANGSTER'S CODE **III**

By **J-Blunt**

KING OF NEW YORK III

By **T.J. Edwards**

CUM FOR ME **IV**

By **Ca$h & Company**

GORILLAS IN THE BAY

De'Kari

THE STREETS ARE CALLING

Duquie Wilson

KINGPIN KILLAZ II

Hood Rich

168

STEADY MOBBIN' **III**

Marcellus Allen

SINS OF A HUSTLER

ASAD

HER MAN, MINE'S TOO **II**

Nicole Goosby

GORILLAZ IN THE BAY **II**

DE'KARI

TRIGGADALE II

Elijah R. Freeman

Available Now

RESTRAINING ORDER **I & II**

By **CA$H & Coffee**

LOVE KNOWS NO BOUNDARIES **I II & III**

By **Coffee**

RAISED AS A GOON I, II, III & IV

BRED BY THE SLUMS I, II, III

BLAST FOR ME I & II

ROTTEN TO THE CORE I III

By **Ghost**

LAY IT DOWN **I & II**

LAST OF A DYING BREED

BLOOD STAINS OF A SHOTTA I & II

By **Jamaica**

LOYAL TO THE GAME

Ghost

LOYAL TO THE GAME II

LOYAL TO THE GAME III

By **TJ & Jelissa**

BLOODY COMMAS I & II

SKI MASK CARTEL I II & III

KING OF NEW YORK I II

By **T.J. Edwards**

IF LOVING HIM IS WRONG…I & II

LOVE ME EVEN WHEN IT HURTS

By **Jelissa**

WHEN THE STREETS CLAP BACK I & II III

By **Jibril Williams**

A DISTINGUISHED THUG STOLE MY HEART I II & III

LOVE SHOULDN'T HURT I II

RENEGADE BOYS

By **Meesha**

A GANGSTER'S CODE I & II

By J-Blunt

PUSH IT TO THE LIMIT

By **Bre' Hayes**

BLOOD OF A BOSS **I, II, III & IV**

By **Askari**

THE STREETS BLEED MURDER **I, II & III**

THE HEART OF A GANGSTA I II& III

By **Jerry Jackson**

CUM FOR ME

CUM FOR ME 2

A Bronx Tale

CUM FOR ME 3

An **LDP Erotica Collaboration**

BRIDE OF A HUSTLA **I II & II**

THE FETTI GIRLS **I, II& III**

CORRUPTED BY A GANGSTA I & II

By **Destiny Skai**

WHEN A GOOD GIRL GOES BAD

By **Adrienne**

A GANGSTER'S REVENGE **I II III & IV**

THE BOSS MAN'S DAUGHTERS

THE BOSS MAN'S DAUGHTERS II

THE BOSSMAN'S DAUGHTERS III

THE BOSSMAN'S DAUGHTERS IV

THE BOSS MAN'S DAUGHTERS **V**

A SAVAGE LOVE **I & II**

BAE BELONGS TO ME

A HUSTLER'S DECEIT I, II

WHAT BAD BITCHES DO I, II

By **Aryanna**

A KINGPIN'S AMBITON

A KINGPIN'S AMBITION **II**

I MURDER FOR THE DOUGH

By **Ambitious**

TRUE SAVAGE

TRUE SAVAGE II

TRUE SAVAGE **III**

TRUE SAVAGE **IV**

171

Ghost

TRUE SAVAGE **V**
By **Chris Green**
A DOPEBOY'S PRAYER
By **Eddie "Wolf" Lee**
THE KING CARTEL **I, II & III**
By **Frank Gresham**
THESE NIGGAS AIN'T LOYAL **I, II & III**
By **Nikki Tee**
GANGSTA SHYT **I II &III**
By **CATO**
THE ULTIMATE BETRAYAL
By **Phoenix**
BOSS'N UP **I , II & III**
By **Royal Nicole**
I LOVE YOU TO DEATH
By Destiny J
I RIDE FOR MY HITTA
I STILL RIDE FOR MY HITTA
By **Misty Holt**
LOVE & CHASIN' PAPER
By **Qay Crockett**
TO DIE IN VAIN
By **ASAD**
BROOKLYN HUSTLAZ
By **Boogsy Morina**
BROOKLYN ON LOCK I & II
By **Sonovia**

172

A Bronx Tale

GANGSTA CITY

By **Teddy Duke**

A DRUG KING AND HIS DIAMOND I & II III

A DOPEMAN'S RICHES

HER MAN, MINE'S TOO

By Nicole Goosby

TRAPHOUSE KING **I II & III**

KINGPIN KILLAZ

By **Hood Rich**

LIPSTICK KILLAH **I, II**

CRIME OF PASSION

By **Mimi**

STEADY MOBBN' **I, II**

By **Marcellus Allen**

WHO SHOT YA **I, II**

Renta

GORILLAZ IN THE BAY

DE'KARI

TRIGGADALE

Elijah R. Freeman

BOOKS BY LDP'S CEO, CA$H

TRUST IN NO MAN

TRUST IN NO MAN 2

TRUST IN NO MAN 3

BONDED BY BLOOD

SHORTY GOT A THUG

THUGS CRY

THUGS CRY 2

THUGS CRY 3

TRUST NO BITCH

TRUST NO BITCH 2

TRUST NO BITCH 3

TIL MY CASKET DROPS

RESTRAINING ORDER

RESTRAINING ORDER 2

IN LOVE WITH A CONVICT

Coming Soon

BONDED BY BLOOD 2

BOW DOWN TO MY GANGSTA

A Bronx Tale

www.ingramcontent.com/pod-product-compliance
Lightning Source LLC
Chambersburg PA
CBHW070033260626
47159CB00005B/2024